PAUL MARCHAND, F. M. C.

PAUL MARCHAND, F. M.C.

Charles W. Chesnutt

Edited with introduction
and notes by
Dean McWilliams

PRINCETON UNIVERSITY PRESS

Library of Congress Cataloging-in-Publication Data

Chesnutt, Charles Waddell, 1858–1932
[Paul Marchand, free man of color]
Paul Marchand, F.M.C. / by Charles W. Chesnutt; edited with
introduction and notes by Dean McWilliams.
p.   cm.   Includes bibliographical references (p.   ).
ISBN 0-691-05993-4 (CL: alk. paper).
ISBN 0-691-05994-2 (PB: alk. paper)
1. Inheritance and succession—Louisiana—New Orleans—Fiction.
2 Passing (Identity)—Louisiana—New Orleans—Fiction.
3. Intermarriage—Louisiana—New Orleans—Fiction.
4. New Orleans (La.)—Race relations—Fiction.
5. White men—Louisiana—New Orleans—Fiction.
I. McWilliams, Dean. II. Title.
PS1292.C6P38 1999   98-26423   813'.4—dc21

This book has been composed in Berkeley Ten
Designed by Jan Lilly

The paper used in this publication
meets the minimum requirements of
ANSI / NISO Z39.48-1992 (R1997) (*Permanence of Paper*)

http://pup.princeton.edu

Printed in the United States of America

2 4 6 8 10 9 7 5 3 1

CONTENTS

INTRODUCTION TO
PAUL MARCHAND, F.M.C.

THE *Norton Anthology of African American Literature* records a common assumption about Charles W. Chesnutt's literary career: "Although he continued writing
and speaking on various social and political issues . . .,
Chesnutt produced only a handful of short stories in
the last twenty-five years of his life" (523). This
assumption is mistaken and deserves correction, for
Chesnutt remained a novelist until the end of his years,
completing two long narratives in the seventh and
eighth decades of his life. Although Chesnutt submitted both manuscripts for publication, neither was
published, and, as a consequence, African American
literary history records an oddly truncated picture of
his literary activity, telling us virtually nothing about
Chesnutt's writings during the last third of his long
career.

Chesnutt was born in 1858 in Cleveland, Ohio,
where his parents, both free Negroes, had migrated
from North Carolina in the late 1850s. Chesnutt's father and mother decided to return to their native state
after the Civil War, and thus Chesnutt spent his late

childhood, adolescence, and early adulthood in the area around Fayetteville, North Carolina. Chesnutt decided, while still in his teens, that he wanted to become a writer, and, with that end in mind, he trained himself in languages and read widely in the world's literature. He was able to support himself as a schoolteacher, but sensing that this profession might not provide an adequate livelihood, he also taught himself stenography. In 1883, after the failure of Reconstruction, Chesnutt found it increasingly difficult to live in the South, so with his wife and children, he moved back to Cleveland. There he read law and passed the state bar with the highest score in his group. Finding his hope of practicing law blocked by racial prejudice, he started a profitable career as a legal stenographer.

Chesnutt had not, however, forgotten his literary aspirations, and in the mid-1880s his stories and sketches began to appear in print. In August 1887 *The Atlantic Monthly* published his story "The Goophered Grapevine," and in 1899 Houghton Mifflin brought out his collection of stories *The Conjure Woman*. These two dates mark signal events in African American literary history. Novels and stories written by black Americans had been published as early as the mid-nineteenth century, but these narratives were primarily polemical in purpose, and they were read and discussed in the context of the national debates on Abolition and Reconstruction. Before Chesnutt's, no fiction written by a Negro had received serious attention from America's white literary establishment. Chesnutt's stories were hailed as fictions of a high order, and the praise was justified, for these stories combined sensitive portraiture of American blacks with considerable literary skill. Chesnutt's historic publications drew the attention of America's literary elite and marked African American fiction's emergence as a literary art form. Chesnutt followed these path-breaking publications quickly with four additional volumes: another story collection, *The Wife of His Youth and Other Stories of the Color Line* (1899), and three novels, *The House Behind the Cedars* (1900), *The Marrow of Tradition* (1901), and *The Colonel's Dream* (1905). And then silence—or so it seemed. Chesnutt published a few essays and several more stories, but there were no more book-length publications before his death in 1932.

It is often thought that the commercial failure of his third novel in 1905 caused Chesnutt to abandon fiction. It is true that Chesnutt was discouraged by his inability to support his family by his writing, and after the disappointing returns on *The Colonel's Dream*, he turned his energies to his practice as a legal stenographer. But he did not give up fiction entirely, and he pursued a number of fictional projects; the most important of these were two novels for which he unsuccessfully sought publication in the 1920s. The first of these, *Paul Marchand, F.M.C.*, is a historical romance set in New Orleans.

The manuscript was returned by three separate pub-

lishers in late 1921, and although we do not have the
rejection letters, we can speculate about the reasons it
was refused. Chesnutt, who had enjoyed only modest
commercial success with his previous publications,
had been off the literary scene for fifteen years. The
Harlem Renaissance would stimulate interest in Negro
writers later in the decade, but this movement was just
getting under way and could do Chesnutt little good in
1921. There was an additional obstacle in that *Paul
Marchand, F.M.C.*, on one level at least, is a local-color
romance. The vogue for this type of fiction, pioneered
by Chesnutt's friend George Washington Cable, had
crested and receded in the late nineteenth century; it
would not have seemed a promising genre to market-
conscious publishers in the 1920s. In any case, the
alacrity of the publishers' responses to Chesnutt's sub-
missions—three refusals in a little over two months—
suggests that the manuscript never received sympathetic attention.

It may be easier for us to appreciate this novel now,
seventy years later, than it was when Chesnutt first
submitted it. Our attitude toward African American
writing is, of course, totally different: artists of African
descent are now among the most important and crea-
tive voices in American letters, and this has spurred
interest in earlier Negro writers. But beyond this, there
have been significant changes in the philosophical
and critical climate. We have become more suspicious
of language, more alert to the ways ideology perme-

ates the structures we use to organize reality. *Paul Marchand, F.M.C.* dramatically illustrates the power of those groups who control the language we use. In this novel, Chesnutt's protagonist finds that his identity has been changed overnight. His race, his name, his family, and even his marital status have been totally transformed by the words of a powerful patriarch and his attorney.

Chesnutt returned in this novel to a theme central to his earlier fiction: the people of mixed racial ancestry. This preoccupation reflects his personal experience as a light-skinned mulatto, but his fictional exploitation of this experience is more than an autobiographical indulgence. The world of the mulatto is the ambiguous area where the arbitrary, socially conditioned nature of racist thinking can be most easily exposed. Racist ideology insists on rigidly exclusive categories: blacks and whites are fundamentally and immutably different, biologically, intellectually, and morally. But the existence of people of mixed blood contradicted assumptions of absolute racial difference; mulattoes were living proof that desire and love had drawn whites and blacks together in ways that revealed their common humanity. Moreover, mulattoes—full Negroes under the law and in racist ideology—often differed little in appearance, behavior, and achievement from whites. Life along the color line, with individuals moving back and forth across a supposedly uncrossable gulf, is a world of slipping signifiers, a world where the artificial, socially and historically conditioned nature of our thinking about race is most evident.

Recent literary theory, in addition to encouraging our suspicion of language and social codes, has helped us understand the complex relationship of black writers to the white literary tradition. Henry Louis Gates Jr.'s *The Signifying Monkey* has shown the relevance of *signifying* to black literary practice, demonstrating how black writers echo, transform, and often subvert, the literary themes of white writers. Critics such as William L. Andrews and Houston Baker have explored the ways that Chesnutt's short fiction recast the stereotypes of white plantation school fiction. A similar awareness of prior white representations of blacks and mulattoes is useful for understanding *Paul Marchand, F.M.C.*, for this is a novel whose "Foreword" self-consciously alludes to the local-color romances of George Washington Cable and Grace King. Chesnutt, who had no firsthand knowledge of Creole culture, drew significantly from these white literary sources, as I have indicated at several points in my notes.

But Chesnutt's relationship to his white predecessors here, as in his conjure tales, is more complex than mere borrowing. Chesnutt's revisionary strategy may be seen in his portrait of the "F.M.C." or "Free Man of Color." The most famous representation of a New Orleans quadroon prior to Chesnutt's novel was Honoré Grandissime, F.M.C., in George Washington Cable's *Grandissimes* (1880). Cable's character was bold for its time, and it stirred angry reactions from Southern reviewers for its imputation of Negro blood in the families of the Creole elite. Nonetheless, Cable's portrait did not escape the stereotypes associated with the person whose blood is fatally mixed: Cable's mulatto is self-absorbed, indecisive and, finally, suicidal. Cable's literary rival Grace Kind made it clear that, for her part, the ideal mulatto was distinguished by his "humble acquiescence in the exigencies of his social position" (347). Chesnutt's hero is neither Cable's tainted weakling nor King's deferential sychophant. Paul Marchand, from the beginning, regards himself as the equal of his white peers. As the novel progresses, he proves his moral superiority to them, growing in self-understanding and in identification with oppressed blacks. In the novel's climax, he frees the slaves he has inherited and stingingly rejects racist Creole society and its privileges. More important than the revisions represented by any particular character, Chesnutt's narrative subverts the essentializing racial distinctions upon which these earlier racial portraits were based. Marchand's racial designation changes and with it the public perception of his moral "essence"; the insulted pariah becomes the envied scion, literally overnight, all at a dying aristocrat's whim.

Paul Marchand, F.M.C was not Chesnutt's only excursion into Louisiana local color. His unpublished short story "The Hand of God," in the Western Historical Society Library, is set among the Creoles of the lower Mississippi. The story is undated, but a revision clipped to the manuscript is written on the back of a bank deposit slip with the printed date "192_." This suggests that Chesnutt was at least revising the story during the 1920s, roughly the time when he was writing *Paul Marchand*. "The Hand of God" is, however, a much more conventional instance of local-color writing than is the novel; this story of a murder and its punishment is strong in atmosphere but lacks the novel's significant social thematics.

Quite apart from Chesnutt's interest in local color, there were other, nonliterary reasons for his fascination with 1820s Louisiana. Despite the remporal distance, Chesnutt's "Foreword" assures his readers that they will find similarities between the narrative's time and their own. He reinforces this point in the novel's last paragraph by linking his story to racial legislation proposed in Louisiana in 1921. To see the connections between the historic and the contemporary and to bring into focus the contradictions that fascinated Chesnutt, we need to sketch briefly several moments in the history of Louisiana race relations. Before the Civil War, Louisiana recognized a tripartite racial schema, with the free mixed-blood population having their own distinct status between Negro and white. After Reconstruction, Louisiana, like the rest of the South, sought to impose a rigid binary system, strictly dividing whites from all individuals with even the slightest trace of African ancestry. The transition from the tripartie paradigm to a binary one was anything but smooth: it involved legal, linguistic, and literary struggles that threatened the notion of racial definitions themselves.

Although marriage crossing any of the three racial categories was proscribed by the 1825 Louisiana Civil Code, miscegenation was common before the Civil War. Post-Reconstruction Louisianans were less tolerant, and they sought to guarantee the purity of the new racial definitions by a 1908 statute making "concubinage between a person of the Caucasian race and a person of the Negro race a felony" (Dominguez 29). However, when this law was enforced against a white man living with an octoroon woman, the Louisiana Supreme Court acquitted the defendants, asserting that an octoroon was a person of color but not a Negro. The 1910 session of the Louisiana state legislature reacted angrily to the court's lenient racial distinctions by passing a new law prohibiting concubinage between a white and a person of the Negro or colored race.

The controversy continued in the next decade, and Chesnutt refers ironically in *Paul Marchand*'s final paragraph to recent legislation introduced into the Louisiana legislature "making marriage a felony between a white person and a person of colored blood to the thirty-second degree inclusive." The *Official Journal* of Louisiana's Tenth Constitutional Convention records that on March 8, 1921, Delos R. Johnson attempted to insert in the Louisiana constitution the stipulation to which Chesnutt refers (Kunkle 19). The effort failed, but the anxious need to define racial identities as precisely and firmly as possible was very much alive in Louisiana during the time Chesnutt was preparing *Paul Marchand.*

So also was the memory of *Plessy vs. Ferguson.* In this celebrated 1896 court case, the United States Supreme Court upheld the constitutionality of the Louisiana law requiring segregation in railroad accommodations. Albion Tourgee, Chesnutt's personal friend, was among the attorneys who brought suit challenging the South's Jim Crow laws. Tourgee and his associates deliberately selected as their litigant Homer Plessy, a Louisiana octoroon. Plessy had been born a free man of color in 1862, and his skin was so light that he had to inform the conductor that he was a Negro in order that he might be arrested. Tourgee's choice of a mulatto litigant was motivated, not by a wish to claim special privileges for light-skinned Negroes, but as an occasion to argue the arbitrary and artificial character of all racial distinctions. This is, of course, the central point and key strategy behind Chesnutt's novel. Homer Plessy's paradoxical situation may well have reminded Chesnutt of the relevance of Louisiana history and custom to the absurdities of contemporary American racial dogma.

Heretofore, the body of Chesnutt's published fiction has stood at six volumes: the five books Chesnutt saw into print and the volume of his previously uncollected stories, which Sylvia Lyons Render edited in 1974.

Charles Hackenberry's recent edition of *Mandy Oxendine* gives us what was probably Chesnutt's first novel. The publication of *Paul Marchand, F.M.C.*, by Princeton University Press and by the University Press of Mississippi, and Chesnutt's last novel, *The Quarry*, by Princeton University Press, expand Chesnutt's published corpus of fiction by nearly a third, extending it through the final decades of his career. The publication of Chesnutt's late novels also changes our appreciation of African American literature during a crucial transitional period. The two decades between the appearance of Chesnutt's *The Colonel's Dream*, in 1905, and the beginning of the Harlem Renaissance in 1924, are generally counted among the least productive for black American writing; "no more than five Afro-Americans had published significant books" (Lewis 89) in these nineteen years. *Paul Marchand, F.M.C.* emerged during this low period. Chesnutt's dark romance catches the dispirited mood of the moment, but its presence reminds us that black writers continued to work through this period, despite the denial of publication.

The only complete manuscript of *Paul Marchand, F.M.C.* is in the Charles W. Chesnutt Collection in Fisk University Library. This manuscript and other Chesnutt materials were donated to Fisk by Chesnutt's daughter Helen Chesnutt. There are also 23 scattered pages of this novel in the Chesnutt Collection in the Western Reserve Historical Society Library in Cleveland. These pages are identical to the corresponding pages in the Fisk manuscript. The Fisk manuscript, 179 pages of double-spaced typed text, is in very good condition. It appears to be the manuscript Chesnutt submitted for publication. In his letter of submission to Alfred Knopf dated December 20, 1921, Chesnutt refers to an incident which occurs in the manuscript on page 177, and that incident occurs on page 177 in the Fisk text. Chesnutt had already submitted the novel to Houghton Mifflin Company on October 8, 1921, and to Harcourt Brace and Company on November 12, 1921. These dates of submission follow so quickly that it is reasonable to assume that Chesnutt was sending on to Knopf the manuscript which had been read and returned by the two other publishers.

I have taken the Fisk manuscript as the basis for my edition of the novel. In editing the manuscript I have treated it as a manuscript submitted for publication, and I have confined myself to correcting inaccuracies and inconsistencies in spelling, grammar, and punctuation. I have explained the most significant of my corrections in my notes at the back of this volume. I have also used footnotes to annotate Chesnutt's borrowings and references.

I have many individuals and institutions to thank for help in bringing these manuscripts to print. First, I wish to thank John Chesnutt Slade, Chesnutt's grandson, for permission to publish the manuscript. I wish also to acknowledge the assistance of the following: Gary Hunt and George Bain of Ohio University's Alden

Library; Beth Howse of Fisk University's Erastus Milo Cravath Memorial Library; Susan Crowl and Vattel Rose of Ohio University, and Michel Perdreaux, formerly of Ohio University; Etienne De Planchard of the Université de Toulouse–Le Mirail; Roy Rosenstein of the American University in Paris; and George Hutchinson of the University of Tennessee. I must also express my gratitude to Ohio University for a Research Committee grant and for a faculty fellowship; this support provided some of the resources and the time from teaching which enabled me to do most of my research. Finally, and most important, I am once again in debt to my wife, Alvi, for her help, encouragement, and unfailing good humor.

I dedicate this edition to my niece and nephew, Holly and Luke Stowell.

PAUL MARCHAND, F. M. C.

FOREWORD

⟹➤●◄⟸

THE VISIT of a French duke to New Orleans, in the early part of the last century, and the social festivities in his honor, are historical incidents. If there was not a Paul Marchand case in New Orleans, there might well have been, for all the elements of such a drama were present, as is clearly set out in the careful studies of life in the old Creole city by Miss Grace King and Mr. George W. Cable,[1] which are available for the student or the general reader—the author has made free reference to them—as well as in the more obscure records and chronicles from which they drew their information. Had there been such a case, it is conceivable that the principal character might, under the same conditions, have acted as did the Marchand of the story.

The quadroon caste vanished with slavery, in which it had its origin. Indeed long before the Civil War it had begun to decline. Even the memory of it is unknown to the present generation, and it is of no interest except to the romancer or the historian, or to the student of sociology, who may discover some interesting parallels between social conditions in that earlier generation and those in our own. Quadroons and octoroons there are in plenty in the New Orleans of today, as any one with a discriminating eye, taking a walk along Canal Street, may plainly see; but as a distinct class they no longer exist. Since all colored people enjoy the same degree of freedom, and are subject to the same restrictions, there are no longer any legal or social distinctions between the descendants of the former free people of color and those of the former slaves. Social decree has made them all Negroes, no doubt to the advancement of democracy among themselves, perhaps to the betterment of public morals, but certainly at the expense of accuracy and the picturesque.

But the Father of the Waters recks not of such trifles and still pursues his stately course beside the Crescent City. The language of Bienville and its local variant are still heard. The roses still riot in the gardens and on the latticed galleries. The old Creole families still cherish their pride of race and their family traditions, and their ladies still retain an enviable reputation for beauty and for charm—to say nothing of their chicken gumbo.

C. W. C.

CHAPTER I

———➤●◄———

In the Vieux Carré

TOWARD THE end of the first quarter of the nineteenth century, New Orleans, the little city planted on the banks of the Mississippi, was in the full tide of a newborn prosperity. Always French at heart, in spite of the successive strains of alien humanity which penetrated and mingled with its population—Spanish, Indian, African, English, Irish, American—it had been nearly a score of years under the government of the United States. Eight or ten years before, General Jackson, defeating the British in a famous battle, had firmly established the American influence, and made the word "Yankee" a symbol of respect, instead of, as formerly, a term of suspicion and reproach. Prosperity had followed the incorporation of the colony into the Republic. From 1812 to 1821 the population had nearly doubled. The Mississippi swarmed with steamboats, laden with cotton and sugar from the up river districts, destined for shipment to Europe or the North. The old city walls had been torn down, the moat filled up and converted into boulevards. From a sleepy, slow, but picturesque provincial French town, with a Spanish veneer, the Crescent City had been swept into the current of American life, and pulsed and throbbed with the energy of the giant young nation of the West.

Nevertheless, these changes were in many respects as yet merely superficial. The great heart of the community—the thoughts, the feelings, the customs, the prejudices, the religion of the people—remained substantially unchanged. The current was swifter, but the water was the same. The Americans, while tolerated socially, were still a class apart, though by virtue of their superior energy and genius for politics they were rapidly becoming the ruling class. The Creoles had their own very proud and exclusive society. They had resented the Spanish dominion; they were not yet quite reconciled to the American occupation. They were the professional men and the owners of land and slaves, the *rentiers*, or gentlemen of independent income.

Descending by easy grades, there were the people of color—octoroons, quadroons, mulattoes—many of them small tradesmen, a few of them large merchants or planters, and more than one the inheritor of substantial means from a white father or grandfather—an inferior but not entirely degraded class. A battalion of free colored men, for instance, had served gallantly in the War of 1812, and had won the praise of the commander-in-chief; while the quadroon women were famous for their beauty and their charm, neither of which could have existed without some friendly encouragement. At the basis of all lay the black slaves, whose arduous and unrequited toil, upon the broad, deep-soiled plantations of indigo, rice, cotton and sugar cane, furnished the wherewithal to maintain the wealth and luxury of the capital.

One day in the spring of 1821, about ten o'clock in the morning an old colored woman entered the *vieux carré*, or old square, with a large basket upon her head, and took up her stand in front of the porch of the Cabildo or Hotel de Ville or City Hall, as it was successively called under the various regimes, the beautiful old Spanish building which still faces the Place d'Armes, now Jackson Square. She placed her basket on the pavement, removed the clean white cotton cloth which covered it, and disposed for exhibition the contents, consisting of *pralines*, or little crisp sweet cakes, a popular Creole delicacy. She then pulled out from behind one of the columns of the porch a three-legged wooden stool, hers by right of property or prescription, and took her seat upon it by the basket.

"*Pralines!* Fresh and sweet! *Pralines, messieurs! Pralines, mesdames! Pralines, mes enfants!*"

Her mellow voice resounded beneath the arches of the porch, and out over the Place d'Armes. The leisurely activities of the city were in full swing. It was about the hour for the courts, and, as it was a feast day in Lent, a second service in the cathedral was to begin shortly. More than one gentleman with a sweet tooth stopped in front of the old woman long enough to purchase one of the crisp cakes, which he munched surreptitiously as he went on. Others dropped a coin into the basket, accepting nothing in return but a bow, a curtsey, or the old woman's voluble thanks. A minor city official, entering the Cabildo, stopped a moment to chaff with the old street vender. The day was warm, the gentleman was stout, and he had removed his hat which he held in his hand.

"*Bonjour, Zabet!*" he said. "You grow younger and younger. You do not look a day over a hundred." Zabet's reputed great age was a popular myth.

"*Bonjour, miché (monsieur). Voulez vous des pralines?* It is hard to determine your age, *Monsieur l'Interprète*, by looking at you. Did you lose your hair from age or early piety?"

The bystanders laughed, and the interpreter, acknowledging his defeat with a shrug and a grimace, entered the building.

An elderly lawyer, with a dignified and imposing mien, attended by a colored servant carrying a briefcase, drew near. He was absorbed in thought and seemed not to observe the old woman's deferential salute. She respected his mood and did not accost him.

"There, my children," she observed sententiously to the group of loiterers about her, "there goes Miché Jules Renard, the great advocate. He is a lawyer for Père Antoine, the rector of the parish, and for the very rich

Miché Pierre Beaurepas. It was not from any lack of courtesy or consideration that he did not speak to me, for he is one of my best friends, but because he has business on his mind of such moment that he can think of nothing else."

A judge went by. To him Zabet bowed as deeply as her seated position and her girth would permit. No native of New Orleans respected authority more than old Zabet Philosophe[1]—as she was called—Elizabeth the wise woman. For twenty-odd years a fixture in the *vieux carré*, she had been a public institution, known and respected of all men, since General Jackson, nine years before, in the full tide of his popularity, had publicly shaken hands with her on the steps of the cathedral, had praised her patriotism, commended the gallantry of the free colored troops, and given Zabet a silver dollar. She had kept the dollar ever since, though often offered for it many times its value. It was a standing joke to try to purchase this souvenir.

The judge nodded to the cake-woman. Zabet gave to her audience details, in Gumbo or Negro French, of the judge's imposing pedigree and the grandeur of his ancestors. When addressing white people she spoke excellent French, having lived the greater part of her life in the houses of the rich and cultured, first in San Domingo, from which she had fled, with her master's children, during the insurrection of 1793, and later in New Orleans, where in recognition of her loyalty, she had for half a century enjoyed the privileges of a free woman. Indeed, her immunity from slavery had lasted so long that her free papers were never asked for—no more than one would have looked for the charter of the city or the title deeds of the Cabildo. She was old, and fat, and brown as old mahogany; but she had once been young and fair and slender, and her wisdom was that of a varied, not to say variegated experience. She had been by turns seamstress, hairdresser, laundress, nurse and midwife, and had become a seller of cakes only when age and rheumatism had disqualified her somewhat from more active pursuits. She was the repository of more than one family secret, and discretion was one of her few virtues.

Shortly after the judge had disappeared within the doorway of the city hall, a Creole gentleman of about thirty, dressed in the European fashion which the Creoles affected, with very high collar, full shirt front and voluminous cravat, top boots with large flaps, and somewhat stouter of build and less open of countenance than most men of his race, approached old Zabet on the way to the Cabildo. To this gentleman, a member of the family which held the dormant title to the old cake-woman—she being, though she had forgotten it, a chattel person—Zabet Philosophe instinctively yielded the deference due his name, and, rising laboriously from her stool, greeted him with a profound curtsey, to which he responded with an absent-minded nod.

"Miché Adolphe seems depressed," suggested the old woman, insinuatingly.

The appearance of the stout gentleman bore out this conjecture. He looked decidedly worried. At the old woman's remark he paused in front of her and sighed.

"I had a dream, last night, Miché Adolphe," she said, "in which you had fallen into the river. You had gone down twice, and were throwing up your hands for the last time."

It was a superstitious age, and Zabet's dreams were an easy expedient, by which she was able to talk to white people with a freedom which would not have been permitted to less privileged colored persons.

"You should not presume to dream of me, old witch, unless your dreams are good ones. No need to predict bad luck—it is mine already!"

"But you are too impatient, master! That was not all my dream. You were rescued at the last moment."

"By whom?" he demanded eagerly.

Zabet Philosophe's dreams had often come true; this had been known to happen many times. The guesses of a shrewd observer, who understands the character and circumstances of those about, may often hit the mark. Moreover Zabet's dreams were often shrewdly calculated, as in this instance, to accomplish indirectly some very definite purpose.

"By your uncle Pierre," she rejoined, "who threw you a plank, *mon Dieu*, upon which you swam safely ashore!"

Adolphe Beaurepas's face lit up with hope. Was this dream of the old mulatress a good omen? Was it at all possible that his close-fisted uncle Pierre would help him to lift the miserable mortgage, ripe for foreclosure, which covered the whole of his small estate?

"Tell me, Zabet!" he said, dropping into the Philosophe's basket one of his few pieces of silver, "do you think he would care to see me?"

"He received you affectionately in my dream," returned Zabet, "which was one of the true kind. I saw Miché Pierre only last night, and he spoke of his dear nephews and of how much he loved them. And he added that he was growing old, and must decide upon his heir."

"Dear, good uncle!" replied Adolphe Beaurepas, with a cunning smile. "He does not know how much I love him. I think I shall pay him a visit."

"By all means," returned Zabet. "I should not neglect it. Out of sight, out of mind."

"*Merci*, Zabet, I'll go and see him."

"Go in the morning, Miché Adolphe, when he is fresh and his mind is clear. You will have a better reception."

The court had not yet opened, but the hour for opening was at hand, and several belated lawyers hurried past with their clients and witnesses. As a gentleman, taller of stature than most Creole men, who as a rule, though athletic, were of about the middle height, passed old Zabet in too great haste to notice her, she called out to him.

"There is no need to hurry, Miché Henri. The judge

has not yet gone in. I was at Miché Pierre's house this morning."

"And how is my uncle?" queried Henri Beaurepas, another of the nephews of the rich Creole proprietor referred to by Zabet.

"Failing, Miché Henri, though he does not seem to realize it."

Standing in the glare of the morning sun, Henri Beaurepas's face showed indubitable marks of dissipation. Late hours do not conduce to early rising or firm cheeks or clear eyes. He had sat in a gambling house on Canal Street until three o'clock that morning, and had suffered heavy losses at cards, for which he had given his notes of hand, payable on demand, thus increasing the total of his debts by several thousand dollars. His expression brightened when the old woman spoke.

"Why do you think he is failing, Zabet?" he asked with restrained eagerness.

"Why, Miché Henri? Because he is thinking of his heir. He asked about you. He spoke very kindly. I think he would like to see you."

Another silver piece dropped into the old woman's basket.

"I'll go and see him, Zabet. When is he in the best humor?"

"I should go just before noon, Miché Henri—before luncheon. He is apt then to be in a pleasant mood. But there comes your judge."

"Then I must hurry in, and finish my testimony. I

am a witness in the Janvier case. *Merci*, Zabet; when I come into the estate, I'll not forget you." The Janvier case was a famous, long drawn out piece of litigation involving the title to a large tract of valuable land.

"*Merci, miché*," said Zabet, with a curtsey, but the smile with which she followed the gentleman as he entered the city hall, had more of shrewd cynicism than of the servility which had marked it when face to face with her interlocutor. Among other things which slavery had taught Zabet, if she needed any instruction, was, when she chose, the ability to so control her features that they did not reveal her thoughts, a very valuable accomplishment for one of her condition.

There was a lull in the street movement for a brief space, and then the bells of the cathedral nearby rang out for morning mass. This venerable and imposing pile, with its mixture of rustic, Tuscan and Roman Doric styles of architecture, its towers lined with low spires, and its arched door with clustered columns on either hand, occupied one side of the old square, and was the recognized center of the Creole life of New Orleans.

As the bells rang out, a shabby one-horse carriage, drawn by a flea-bitten gray gelding, which, in spite of its age, showed signs of breeding, entered the square from St. Anne Street, and passing old Zabet, who dropped an unnoticed curtsey to the occupants, drew up in front of the cathedral door. From it dismounted an elderly Spaniard, with the pointed Velasquez beard affected by men of his race. He was followed by a young woman of rare beauty, whom he assisted to alight. They might have been, as they were in fact, father and daughter.

Zabet, who stood not far from the door of the church, with her eyes fixed upon the couple, did not, for the moment, perceive two gentlemen who were approaching on the street from opposite directions. Each of these, it seemed, was also intent upon the pair in front of the cathedral, and neither perceived the other until they came into personal contact, though with no great degree of violence, for both were walking slowly, immediately in front of the old cake merchant.

One of the two, a handsome young man, of about the middle height, with a proud expression, tinged with a melancholy discontent, had drawn back deprecatingly, and was lifting his hat with a murmured apology, when the other, with a truculent air, drew back his arm almost involuntarily, and struck the first a stinging blow upon the cheek.

"You should stick to the gutter, *canaille*, if you cannot keep out of the way of gentlemen! If you kept your eyes in front of you, instead of staring insolently at white ladies, it would be the better for you. This is not your first offense. You will need more than one lesson to teach you your place."

The person thus addressed, who was apparently no more responsible for the accident than the speaker, turned white at first—whether with fear or anger—but almost instantly the tide of blood flowed back and flushed his cheek a dark crimson, and from his black eyes blazed the fierce resentment to which the blow had given rise. Such of the bystanders as did not know the two men, held their breath for a moment, in anticipation of the tragedy which would in all probability follow so grievous an insult. The men of New Orleans were hot-blooded and impulsive, prone to act first and think afterwards, if the matter demanded thought. Among the Creole French and Spaniards the point of honor was jealously guarded, and frequent resort was had to the code for its maintenance, while among the American adventurers who came down the Mississippi were many violent men who had sought the city because of its distance from courts where their presence was urgently desired. Only the week before, a prominent citizen had been shot down for a less offense than a blow or running into another, and brawls between commoner men were of frequent occurrence.

To the surprise and disappointment of the bystanders, however, the man who had been struck, after a visible effort to restrain himself, made no reply, but merely turned upon his heel and walked quietly away. Around the next corner, however, in a quiet street where he was out of sight and hearing, he first relieved his mind by a flow of strong language which he muttered under his breath, accompanied by gestures significative of defiance and revenge, and then, after this harmless and somewhat childish though perfectly natural performance, drew from his pocket a set of tablets, glanced at the clock in the cathedral nearby, and made a careful memorandum with the gold lead pencil which dangled from his watch chain.

"It is an interesting record," he muttered, running his eye over the page, "and when the credit entries are made, it will be more interesting still. My time will come—I feel it! I am free born—I am rich—I am as white as they; and I have been better educated. Yet they treat me like a Negro, and when I am struck I cannot return the blow, under pain of losing my liberty or my life. Ah, could I but face them as man to man!" he cried, putting his hand to his side, upon an imaginary sword hilt. "But I forget—*nom de Dieu*—a man of color cannot bear arms! But we shall see! We shall see!"

"What insolence!" cried old Zabet, insinuatingly, as the other gentleman, maintaining his position upon the sidewalk, still stared across toward the cathedral door into which the Spaniard and his daughter were disappearing.

The gentleman, absorbed in his own thoughts, made no reply.

"What heavenly beauty, Monsieur Raoul!" crooned the old woman. The young man glanced at the speaker. The white girl had gone in, and the old brown woman offered a ready foil to her radiant youth and beauty. Nevertheless his irritation had not yet subsided, and he only scowled at the old cake woman.

"If only justice were done, Monsieur Raoul," Zabet,

intent upon her own purpose, persisted, "and you, as the eldest born, were acknowledged as your uncle's heir, and you would not have to look at her from a distance. I saw old Miché Pierre this morning. He is in a bad way, poor man!"

"How so, Zabet?" demanded the gentleman, his brow clearing somewhat at the old woman's words. "Is it his heart, or his gout, or both together?"

Zabet shook her head with a portentous sigh.

"His gout, Monsieur Raoul, is threatening his heart. And his spirits are low. He complains that his nephews do not love him, that they neglect their old uncle, that they seldom come near him." Raoul Beaurepas, sugar and cotton broker, roué and speculator, who had just received a call for additional margins to save him from a loss which threatened bankruptcy, jumped at the hook, like a hungry fish at a fat worm. Another silver piece found lodgment in Zabet's basket. The younger Beaurepas were prodigal, while their money lasted.

"*Merci,* Zabet, he shall no longer complain. When is he in the most amiable mood?"

"In the afternoon, Monsieur Raoul, after his siesta, you will make a better impression."

CHAPTER II

————⟫●⟪————

The Prophecy

Flushed with prosperity, Zabet began to give away cakes to several little half-naked pot-bellied black children who were eyeing her basket wistfully. This altruistic pastime was interrupted by the return of the young man who had received the blow from Raoul Beaurepas.

With downcast eyes, and looking neither to right nor left, he was passing old Zabet without looking at her, when he heard himself called, in insinuating tones:

"Oh, miché—Monsieur Marchand—oh, master!"

The young man thus accosted, who was known as Paul Marchand, hesitated. The old woman had witnessed his humiliation, but her form of address was music to the quadroon ear. He turned and approached her.

"What is it, Tante Zabet?"

"I dreamed about you last night, miché."

"You dream too much, Tante Zabet—about things which do not concern you."

"But, miché, it was a beautiful dream. If it came true, it would make you very happy."

"Who says I am not happy?"

"Ah, miché how can you be happy? Did I not see just now? Do I not know?"

"I have wealth."

"Small wealth, Miché! Old Pierre Beaurepas has ten times as much."

"It is enough, and more than most. I have a beautiful wife who loves me dearly, and whom I love no less."

"She is a quadroon, monsieur, and you are white, at least to look at—you could pass for white. You have no mark of color—you could have been a gentleman, monsieur! There are others no whiter!"

Marchand sighed. He had married for love, and his wife had brought him wealth from her white father—a dozen houses, a ship, a warehouse stocked with merchandise, and money in the funds. Marchand loved Julie very deeply. What old Zabet had said was true— he might have passed for white, had he so chosen in time. His paternity he did not know. His mother he had never seen; she had died, he understood, in his infancy. He had been brought up by an elderly quadroon woman, one Angeline Dufour, and his support had been provided by a lawyer of the city, a certain Monsieur Jules Renard, a well known Creole advocate, with a large practice in the French quarter. Monsieur Renard had never acknowledged the paternity of young Marchand, nor indeed had it ever been attributed to him. When questioned once by the lad upon the subject, he had answered somewhat curtly, that Marchand should take the gifts the gods provided, and be thankful and not curious; that his support came from a fund, left to him, Monsieur Renard, as trustee, by a philanthropic gentleman who had known his mother many years before. With this Marchand was forced to be content. That he had not been born in wedlock, as he naturally assumed, gave him little concern; no quadroon was, except in marriage between members of his own class, and he was not the fruit of such a union, and what was shared by all was not a source of shame or disgrace, which are always grounded in some departure from the normal. And in that day there were great men of irregular birth. Many escutcheons of the aristocracy of Europe were crossed by the bar sinister. The Latin mind has ever been tender toward the sins of love and youth and hot blood, and correspondingly merciful toward their fruit. The strain of African blood was infinitely more damning— it could never, in Louisiana, be lived down, unless its possessor should, where possible, leave the neighborhood where he was reared, and, to use an expression still in vogue in our own day, pass for white.

The trust fund administered by Monsieur Renard had fed and clothed young Marchand, had sent him, when he approached manhood, to school in Paris, where he had spent several happy years, finding, in the free atmosphere of student life in the French capital, the opportunity to expand in mind and spirit. There was no color line in France, nor ever has been, and in that country men of color even at that epoch had occasionally distinguished themselves in war, in art, in letters and in politics. His schooling completed, he had remained in Paris until, at the suggestion of Monsieur Renard, he had returned to New Orleans.

Among the passengers of the voyage homeward was Julie Lenoir, the quadroon daughter of Jacques Lenoir, a wealthy New Orleans Creole, by a beloved mistress. Old Lenoir had never married, and upon his death, which had occurred while Julie was still a pupil at the convent in Paris, where she had been sent for her education, had left his entire fortune to his daughter Julie and her younger sister Lizette.

In Paris Julie and Paul had met no difference in treatment because of their color, but when they set foot on an American ship, their origin being known, they were left almost entirely to themselves by the other passengers and therefore instinctively fell back upon each other for companionship during the long voyage. It was before the advent of the steamboat and a sailing vessel consumed from three to six weeks in crossing the Atlantic. Youth, propinquity, sympathy, had their innings, with the result that the two young people fell in love and were married shortly after the vessel arrived at New Orleans.

The care of his wife's property, which under his capable management was rapidly increasing in value, had furnished Marchand with wholesome occupation, and he could have remained in New Orleans indefinitely, to his financial profit, had it not been for the conditions under which he, like others of his kind, were obliged to live, of which his treatment by Raoul Beaurepas on the street in front of the cathedral was an illustration,[1] although an aggravated one, and for which his sojourn in France had entirely unfitted him. No white man had ever struck him before; perhaps none would ever strike him again; but that it could be done, and he could not resent it, were gall and wormwood to him.

Endowed with an energy and an initiative which, had he been entirely white, would have rendered him notable among the easygoing Creoles, he had found it difficult to keep strictly within the lines prescribed for those of his caste, and had at times presumed upon the fairness of his complexion to exercise, in company where he was not known, privileges reserved by law or custom for white men only. Under the old Spanish and French regimes, this might have been done with comparative ease, but, with the American annexation and the ensuing influx of Americans from other states, there had come a hardening of racial lines, and a growing intolerance toward the free colored population. A group of young men, American and Creole, among whom several of the Beaurepas cousins were prominent, had constituted themselves champions of the white race and were always on the alert to rebuke presumption on the part of any mulatto or quadroon. Thus it was almost inevitable that Paul Marchand, by his foreign education and his wife's wealth the most conspicuous young man of his class in the city, and with the proud and sensitive spirit he had inherited from some unknown ancestor, should at some time or other come in contact with one or the other of the Beaurepas, and, with the tremendous odds against him, equally certain that he should have the worst of any such encounter.

"You are no prophet, Zabet," said Marchand, "if you can only tell me what might have been. You can tell me nothing that I do not know already. I have wealth, health, youth, a good education, a loving wife, and I have two bright and beautiful children, than whom there are none lovelier."

"Whom you cannot send to the Ursuline Convent, who cannot sit in a box at the Opera. Your children should be sought after, monsieur, by the best in the land. They will be, no doubt, but not as you would wish."

"*Tais-toi!* Be silent, old croaker! I have had enough to bear for one day, and I have affairs to attend to."

"Tarry a moment, monsieur—master—and I will tell your fortune, as I saw it in a dream—only last night—I swear it! It was an auspicious fortune. Be patient for a moment; I am growing old, and my memory is not what it was." She paused significantly.

"Hurry, old woman, with your nonsense! This will refresh your memory." He tossed a piece of silver into Zabet's basket.

"*Bien merci, miché!* God prosper you! It will buy liniment for my rheumatism. This is your fortune. You are rich, you shall be richer. You are proud, you shall be prouder. You are white, you shall be whiter. You have a handsome wife, you shall have one more beautiful. You have lovely children; you shall have others more lovely. And—you have been insulted, you shall be avenged!"

The quadroon smiled sadly.

"Your dream is only a dream, Zabet!" he said, "and for the most part not a pleasant dream. I hope to be richer, of course, if my affairs are successful—that goes without saying. I can be no whiter, for I could not be born again, and if I could a man may not choose his color. There is no place for pride, and little for self respect, in a quadroon's life. Your dream would make me lose my wife, and there is no better wife in New Orleans. But you have promised me revenge, Zabet, and for that I should like to believe at least that much, of your prophecy, for I myself have dreamed of it."

"It will all come true, miché. There are dreams and dreams, and this is a true one—a prophecy, a revelation—you may trust old Zabet. *Adieu, miché! Merci, miché!*"

The young man had tossed another coin into her basket as he moved away.

The brief service in the cathedral was over by this time, and the congregation dispersing. Among the first to come out, having been of the last to enter and therefore among those seated nearest the door, were the old Spaniard and his beautiful daughter. The gentleman helped the girl into the carriage; and following her, took the reins from the colored lad who had been holding them, to whom he gave a small copper coin, which was immediately spent with Zabet for sweet cakes. The Spaniard's horse, a superannuated thoroughbred, started forward at a leisurely pace.

A singularly graceful young man, of the Creole type, at the same moment entered the square at the side opposite that from which the Spaniard's carriage was leaving. At sight of the vehicle, he quickened his pace to a run and followed it.

"Miché Philippe! Miché Philippe!" called old Zabet after him. But he was gone.

The old cake woman threw a softened look after him.

"There he goes," she muttered, "after old José Morales and his beautiful daughter. He does not like me, Miché Philippe, but I pray for him every night, and I have promised ten candles to St. Anne if she will keep him from harm, and make Miché Pierre leave him a fortune."

Upon leaving old Zabet, Paul Marchand turned the

next corner, and pursued his way along the Rue Toulouse, until he came to a small brick house, with its end
to the street, a balcony overhead, and a door at the side
leading through a brick wall into a garden from which
admittance was gained to the house. It was the residence and *atelier* of Guillaume Perigord, the most popular *maître d'armes* or fencing master of the day, under
whose tuition the gilded youth of New Orleans studied
the use of the rapier and the etiquette of the duello, a
relic of the feudal system which still remained a popular pastime and was destined to linger yet a while.

The young man knocked at the gate, which was
opened by a black servant. A broad-shouldered, athletic Frenchman, somewhat under the medium height,
with fierce mustachios and bristling black hair sprin-
kled with gray, came forward with every evidence of
cordiality.

"*Bonjour, Monsieur Marchand! Comment ça va?* I hope
you carry yourself well today," he exclaimed warmly.

"Miserably, Perigord. I have been insulted by a
blackguard—a *soi-disant* gentleman."

"And you wish me to act as your second? You will
run him through?"

"No, Perigord, this is not Paris. There I was a free
man, a gentleman. Here I am a quadroon—a man of
color—without rights that a white man is bound to
respect."

"*Pardieu, monsieur,* I believe it is so, but, it is a
shame! A great shame! *Sacré nom d'un chien!* You

should go back to Paris, monsieur, where a man is a man. I learned the *art d'escrime* from the mulatto Chevalier St. Georges, the finest fencing master of Paris, the friend of the Regent and of Madame. I fought in Egypt under General Dumas, the hero of the Tyrol, the mulatto friend of Napoleon. They were better men than these who flout you, monsieur."

"Thank you, Perigord. They lived in France, where they could be men. When can you come to my house?"

"Whenever you say, except during my business hours. But why cannot monsieur have his practice here? I can teach you nothing but a trick or two. My Paris predecessor has made you already the best swordsman in New Orleans."

"You flatter me, Perigord. I cannot stand up against you, and I wish to keep up and to improve my skill. You had better come to my house. It would do you no good to have it known that you taught a quadroon an art which he is forbidden by law to exercise. At five o'clock, at my house, by the garden gate. *Au revoir*, Perigord."

Marchand went away.

"He is a great fool," remarked Perigord, lighting a long black cigar. "He is a great fool to stay here, when he has money and could live in France. But Louisiana is full of fools. The grandsons of adventurers and *filles à la cassette* who people Louisiana, look down upon me, the grandson of a marquis and a veteran of the

Grand Army. A wise man would be lonesome in Louisiana."

A few days after the events in the *vieux carré* above recorded, the quadroon Marchand had an altercation, at the cotton exchange, which might have had consequences which would have put an end to all of his problems by putting an end to Marchand himself.

It was the outgrowth, in effect, of old Zabet's dream, which seemed, for a while, by way of bringing in its train the greatest of ill fortune—for the reason, no doubt, that dreams go by contraries. Rolling under his tongue like a sweet morsel the old woman's prophecy—which he had enjoyed without at all believing in it—he had for the time being almost forgotten that he was a quadroon, and that the path which he must walk, in his intercourse with white men, was a straight and narrow one, from which he must deviate neither to the right nor to the left. He was bidding one day for some cotton on the exchange, with which to complete a consignment to his factor in Liverpool. It had been knocked down to his bid, when Hector Beaurepas, who had been bidding against him, claimed the bid as his own. Marchand protested with more heat than prudence.

"I beg your pardon, monsieur," he said, "the bid was mine."

"It was mine," declared Beaurepas rudely. "The auctioneer knows it was mine."

The auctioneer hesitated. He knew it was Marchand's bid, but the controversy was that of quadroon with white man. Marchand saw him wavering.

"It was mine," he insisted. "The gentleman knows it was mine."

Beaurepas made a movement as if to draw the blade from the sword-cane which he carried, but did not complete it.

"*Cochon!*" he cried, "pig of a Negro! Would you call me a liar? The bid was mine and the auctioneer will so declare it. I should like to slit your ears, if it would not soil my sword. It might improve your hearing."

"It is an outrage," murmured one man to another. "It was Marchand's bid."

"It was not the conduct of a gentleman," responded the man addressed. "*Noblesse oblige*, when the other is without redress."

But their remarks, which might have served somewhat as balm to Marchand's wounded spirit, were not spoken in his hearing, and meantime, filled with mortification and with futile rage, he had turned away, with a very poor attempt at dignity. For how could any man, unless he were a hero, or a martyr to a cause— and Marchand was neither—how could anyone move with dignity among those in whose presence he had just been called a pig and been threatened with having his ears slit? Nay, they had even heard it announced that merely to touch him would be a pollution, if but for the purpose of performing upon him a surgical operation, which even a gentleman might presumably perform upon a pig without defilement. How, when the conditions were such, could he not resent the insult?[2]

Poor Marchand! It was a hard world, and only some strain in his nature, odd for one of his upbringing, saved him from self-pity, the most unmanly of sentiments. Consumed with rage, he could only suffer in silence. He could not find relief by speaking to any white Creole, for however much some of them might have sympathized with him, they could not have taken his part without a breach of caste. Marchand would not take his grievance to his colored friends; he would not care to have them know that he had been so humiliated. Instinctively he held himself a little above all but a few of them. Moreover, they would not have understood the intensity of his feeling. They were even more easygoing than their white neighbors, adding to the Creole lack of energy the even greater languor of the African. They were philosophical enough to recognize the existence of facts as they were, and to conform to them as the price of life and some degree of comfort. Indeed some of them already regarded Marchand as a not altogether safe representative of their class, who was likely, by his truculence, to stir up feeling against the rest of them. So Marchand could only rage to his wife, Julie, and find in her sweet sympathy such solace as he might, and make another entry on his tablets, in large letters, heavily underscored.

CHAPTER III

———◦———

Monsieur Pierre Beaurepas

WHEN ADOLPHE BEAUREPAS, following the suggestion made by Zabet Philosophe the day before, ascended the steps of his uncle's mansion the next morning about ten o'clock, his bosom was fluttering with hope. His uncle's house, the temple of the Beaurepas cult, stood on Royal Street, a block from the Place d'Armes and a little to the south of the cathedral. It had been built by Antoine Beaurepas, the father of Pierre, of limestone brought from France in his own bottoms, with a tiled roof, a vaulted entrance leading to a large paved court surrounded by broad galleries or verandahs with wrought-iron railings—perhaps the finest example in the city of the older style of architecture, destined in the newer American section across Canal Street, to give way ere long to the so-called Colonial style, with its Ionic or Corinthian columns, which afterwards became so common in the Southern states.

A dignified, elderly mulatto admitted Adolphe, who

spoke kindly to the servant, his uncle's butler, facto-tum and favorite—a good friend to have at court.

"Good morning, Terence. I hope you are well?"

"Passably well, Miché Adolphe."

"And my excellent uncle—I am sure you take good care of him?"

"He does not complain of me, sir."

"I should like to pay him my respects, Terence. By the way, I know you like a good cigar. These are pure Cubanos, worth their weight in silver."

The butler bowed, and bestowed the cigar carefully in his vest pocket.

"*Merci, Miché Adolphe.* I will announce you."

Adolphe, left alone in the hall, threw around him a look of hungry interest. The polished floor was dotted with costly Persian rugs. The walls of the spacious apartment were hung in part with fine reproductions, in the Aubusson weave, of the set of Gobelin tapestries illustrating episodes in the life of Alexander the Great. The ceiling was a fresco, after Boucher, of the Judg-ment of Paris. On one side a famous Velasquez looked down at him, there was a painting by Vigée Lebrun, and, among other family portraits, one of old Pierre himself, painted by David during the rich colonial's frequent visits to Paris in former years. The furniture was Louis Quinze. There was a large Boulle cabinet, in ebony, on which stood a silver casket, the handiwork of Benvenuto Cellini, flanked by several rare seven-teenth-century bronzes. It was the abode of wealth informed by culture and refined by taste, though there was a noticeable absence of the feminine touch, for old Pierre Beaurepas was a widower of long standing. He had married for love, in middle life, under somewhat romantic circumstances, and when, after some years, his wife, whose slightest whim had been law to one of the hardest men in New Orleans in his dealing with other men, died and left him childless, he remained faithful to her memory and never sought to fill her place. Old Terence, though a slave, a man of capacity and fair education, with a staff of male and female subordinates, conducted the establishment in accordance with the habits and wishes of his master.

Adolphe, waiting, appraised the paintings, the tapestries, and the furniture, with which he was very familiar, having been brought up among them, and imagined himself the owner. He could live very comfortably in the midst of them, or find a use for the money they would bring, should he be lucky enough to be his uncle's heir.

Terence returned ere long.

"The master will see you, sir. Follow me."

The library, into which the servant led the way, was a large room behind the salon, looking out upon the paved courtyard. The walls were lined with glazed bookcases, filled with leather-backed books, many of them bound in hand tooled morocco. There were some choice etchings and wood engravings, and, on a mahogany pedestal a reduced copy, in bronze, of Houdon's seated statue of Voltaire. Adolphe knew the books by their titles, but had small familiarity with their contents; he had never been fond of reading. Many of them, he was aware, were rare and curious, and should they become his, they could readily be turned into money which would buy pleasures he would appreciate far more than those of the intellect.

The old gentleman into whose presence Adolphe Beaurepas was ushered, and whom he saluted with every outward sign of affection and reverence, was seated in an armchair beside an open window. Old and ailing as he was, in the well-cut nose, the high and slightly receding forehead, crowned by a profusion of white hair which fell to his shoulders, the strong chin, which was clean shaven, the thin lips and high cheek bones, the grey eyes, of which age had but slightly dimmed the luster, Adolphe could see the wreck of the virile, capable man of affairs, the disciple of Rousseau and Voltaire, cynical in his attitude toward life, none too trustful of his fellow men, that Pierre Beaurepas had been in his prime. He displayed in his old age, to those with whom he came in contact, that air of assured position, or perhaps assured possessions, which comes to those who have been successful and retain the fruits of success. At his elbow stood a small table, upon which were a flask of Chambertin, a meerschaum pipe, a bowl of tobacco, and a manual of chess, in French. In his hand he held a copy of *Emile*, autographed and annotated by the great Jean Jacques him-

self, which Beaurepas had received from his Parisian
bookseller only the day before—a rare item for his collection. Old Pierre Beaurepas was the wealthiest Creole
in New Orleans. His ancestor, Count Armand de Beaurepas, had helped Bienville to lay the foundations of
the colony, and had profited by valuable land grants
and trading monopolies. A later Beaurepas had been in
Paris at the height of John Law's colossal speculation.
A prudent man, and better informed than most Euro-
peans of the real resources of the colony, he held his
tongue, bought shares in the Mississippi Company,
sold before the bubble burst, and realized five hundred
percent on his investment. Several citizens of Paris,
who claimed that they had been advised by him to in-
vest in Law's scheme, expressed themselves, after the
disaster, with considerable ferocity concerning the colonial Beaurepas and what they would like to do to
him; but since the gentleman, with commendable prudence, had already returned to his home beyond the
seas, their objurgations fell upon the empty air. At the
time of our story the Beaurepas estate, by successive
accretions, due to conservative management, natural
growth and wise and fortunate investments had at-
tained large proportions. By a family custom, based on
feudal tradition, following the law of primogeniture,
the bulk of the estate had always passed to the eldest
son or male representative. But since the American occupation and its attendant changes, the old Creole customs had shown a tendency to relax, and whether the

traditional succession of the Beaurepas estate would be at all altered upon the death of old Pierre, was a question of great importance to several citizens of New Orleans, for more than one reason, the chief of these being that old Pierre Beaurepas was childless, and possessed, therefore, no direct heir.

The succession lay among his five nephews. Pierre had married, at forty, the childless widow of Maxime Ledoux, a friend of his youth, and at one time his partner in business. The lady's second marriage proved no more fruitful than her first. Pierre Beaurepas had had two younger brothers, René and Louis, who owned estates in Haiti, the fairest and the richest of the French colonies. Prior to the revolution in that unhappy island they had lived in luxury upon their revenues. The two brothers and their wives had been massacred, with most of the other whites of the island. Their children, two of one brother and three of the other, had escaped only through the devotion of their colored nurse, Zabet, who had also tried to save the parents, but in vain. She had fled with other refugees, and after incredible hardships had reached New Orleans, where she had turned over to Pierre Beaurepas the children, as the sole survivors of the Haitian branch of the family, and herself, as the sole remnant of the Haitian estates. Since that time, while she had never received any formal deed of manumission, on the other hand, no steps had been taken to administer her as part of the estate of the deceased Haitian Beaurepas, and she had re-

mained, in recognition of her services, to all intents
and purposes a free woman—at any rate a masterless
slave—a sort of human *chose en action*, which had
never been reduced to possession. She could not have
proved her freedom; nor, on the other hand, had anyone ever claimed her as a slave.

Old Pierre Beaurepas had acquitted himself generously toward his orphan nephews. They were brought
up in the house on Royal Street. They were sent to
good schools, and each one, upon reaching his majority, was given sufficient money to set himself up in the
business of his choice, well-fortified in addition by
their uncle's example and his oft repeated precepts. No
one of them had ever been named or suggested as the
heir. Perhaps this very fact was in large measure responsible for the further fact that not one of them had
made a brilliant success in business. Had old Pierre
specifically designated any one of his nephews as his
successor, the remaining four would in all likelihood
have applied their fair native abilities to business with
the hope of finding through this channel the way to
wealth and honors. But how could one reasonably expect a Creole, of Gallic blood and imagination, softened by the languors of a subtropical climate, to struggle painfully toward the heights of life, while there was
one chance in five that he might ride thither in a golden
chariot, behind a black driver in livery?

Old Pierre had fostered no such illusion on the part

of his nephews. On the contrary, he had distinctly informed each of them, upon establishing him in business, that he must make his own way and that the money thus given must not be regarded as an advance upon any future inheritance. But Pierre Beaurepas was eccentric, and supposed not always to mean everything that he said. Moreover, such a statement could not be accepted as conclusive. It was clear that someone must inherit the estate. It was equally obvious that the estate must descend to a Beaurepas, and that there were no possible heirs except the five nephews of the present owner. There was enough to have made them all rich, though it was not conceivable that the estate would be divided.

Without spending a great deal of time, however, in discussing the psychology of the situation, it is nevertheless true that upon this pleasant day when Adolphe Beaurepas entered his uncle's house, the plantation of which he was the nominal owner was mortgaged to the limit of its security value, with foreclosure imminent; that Raoul Beaurepas had used the funds of his firm for his own purposes and was threatened with exposure, unless a miracle should happen; that the business house of which Hector Beaurepas was the head was on the verge of bankruptcy; that Henri Beaurepas owed more debts than he could ever hope to pay out of his income; and when it is borne in mind that old Pierre Beaurepas was in feeble health, his heart action weak, and his gout severe; and when it is further considered that no one of his nephews dared to approach him for aid, for fear that such a step might jeopardize his heirship, it is clearly apparent that there was occasion for considerable anxiety in the minds of the younger Beaurepas. The uncertainty of the situation was sufficient, however, to give them a desperate hold upon solvency—each one was able to inspire his creditors with some of his own hopefulness, and to pacify them pending the outcome of their uncle's illness.

The rainbow of hope had appeared faintly upon Adolphe Beaurepas's financial horizon during his interview with Zabet Philosophe in the morning. During the few hours which had elapsed before his visit to his uncle's house, the arc of promise had grown more and more distinct; and when, upon being ushered into his uncle's presence, old Pierre greeted his nephew with outstretched hand and a contortion of the facial muscles which might have been analyzed, by those who knew the grim old Creole, as something akin to a smile, Adolphe felt a sudden elation inspiring in its quality. The rainbow had led him to the pot of gold.

Old Pierre had not risen from his armchair. His swollen foot, thickly swathed in bandages, rested upon a cushioned footstool. After a first shrewd glance at his nephew, who had greeted him with ceremonious deference, he then, without further preliminaries, demanded of Adolphe how his business was progressing, and whether he could be of any service to him.

Adolphe took heart of courage. That his uncle should manifest this special interest in him was extremely significant. That his uncle should already have informed himself concerning his affairs was quite likely. But if his uncle were ignorant, would it be wise to deceive him, thereby hoping to win a reputation for business acumen which might commend him to his uncle? His uncle might wish to leave the Beaurepas estate in the hands of a successful businessman, by whom he might feel sure it would be wisely administered. But on the other hand, should his uncle discover the deceit which had been practiced upon him, which he could easily do if he wished, the consequences might prove disastrous. No, his uncle Pierre evidently felt a personal interest, a hitherto dormant affection waking into activity toward his favorite nephew, Adolphe. This was a time for frank confession; not too frank, of course—his uncle did not need to know that his embarrassment had been brought about by a reckless speculation; he might be left to infer that it was the result of conditions beyond his nephew's control.

Adolphe told his story. His affairs were prosperous; his prospects were more than fair; but there had been unforseen complications, which he referred to somewhat vaguely—to his relief his uncle did not press him for details; a temporary loan, which he hoped to negotiate somewhere, would tide him over his difficulties.

Old Pierre listened with imperturbable gravity. Adolphe, charmed by his uncle's receptiveness, and engrossed in the construction of a work of fiction, did not observe the old man's eye reading him through and through. It would have taken a more accomplished liar than Adolphe Beaurepas to deceive this veteran of the marketplace.

"And how much, my dear Adolphe," he demanded softly, "would be required to relieve you from this temporary embarrassment?"

Adolphe's inward glow at this inquiry was reflected in his beaming countenance. He had come expecting at least a lecture, instead of which he was offered a loan. He indulged in a moment of rapid reflection. His uncle had practically handed him a blank check. He needed about ten thousand dollars. If he asked for twenty thousand it might be too much. In the middle path there was safety.

"About fifteen thousand dollars, my dear uncle, carefully employed, would carry me well over my present difficulties."

"Ah, well, Adolphe," returned the old gentleman, "to one of my age the sole remaining source of happiness is to make others happy. Some day, perhaps not many years hence, I must die, and my estate must have an heir. I do not wish the name of Beaurepas to be discredited. The man who would inherit my estate must keep his financial honor unsullied."

He rang the silver bell which stood upon the table by his side. His mulatto servant appeared.

"Terence, my check book."

The servant brought the book, and old Pierre drew a check on the Bank of New Orleans for fifteen thousand dollars, to the order of Adolphe Beaurepas.

"You might give me," said the uncle, "a written acknowledgment. It is, of course, between us a mere formality. But an old man cannot change the business habits of a lifetime. An ordinary promissory note will be sufficient."

"Within what time shall I make it be payable?"

"A year?" suggested his uncle.

Adolphe reflected. His uncle could not last three months, six months would leave a wide margin of safety. The more transitory his difficulties were made to seem, the better the impression would remain.

"We can easily repay the loan within six months," he said, "I will make the note for that period."

He thanked his uncle profusely and took his departure, fully convinced he would be the Beaurepas heir, and that the fifteen thousand dollars was merely a pitiful advance upon a great inheritance.

As Adolphe passed through the gate, into the street, he met Zabet Philosophe entering with her basket upon her head.

"*Bonjour, Miché Adolphe*," she said, dropping him a curtsey.

"*Bonjour, Zabet*," said Adolphe, beaming upon the old woman. "Your dream has come true. You are a wise old witch. Here is a dollar for you."

He tossed the coin toward the old woman and went his way, absorbed in dreams of wealth and grandeur. The money fell upon the ground. Zabet stopped somewhat stiffly, picked it up with some difficulty, and dropped it in her capacious pocket. It would buy her another lottery ticket and give her another chance at the capital prize. Then, depositing her basket in the yard, she entered the house and was shown into the old man's presence.

"Adolphe has just left me," he said.

"Yes, master, I met him at the door."

"Have you seen them all, Zabet?" he demanded.

"Yes, master, the rest will all be here. I have seen to it that they shall."

"Do you ever see the young man, Marchand, Zabet?"

"Yes, master."

"Is he well?"

"Perfectly well, Master Pierre."

"And successful in his affairs?"

"Quite so. He seems to have rare good fortune."

"Is he happy?"

The old woman shrugged her shoulders. "How could he be happy, Master Pierre, in New Orleans?"

She related to the old man the scene on the *vieux carré* in which Marchand and Raoul Beaurepas had taken part.

The old man frowned.

"Raoul has a bad temper," he observed. "I fear he is not quite a gentleman. I suspect he associates too freely with the *sacrés américains* who infest our city. No Creole of the older generation would have done such a thing. But advise the young man, when you find occasion, to be patient and to do nothing rash. His case may seem a hopeless one, but miracles have been known to happen. And let me know at once if he should get into any serious difficulty."

"*Très bien, Miché Pierre*, I shall watch him closely."

Before the close of the day, the four Beaurepas cousins to whom Zabet had spoken on the *vieux carré* had called upon their uncle. What happened with Adolphe we have already seen. To each of the others old Pierre gave as seemingly cordial a reception. Each was encouraged to disclose the state of his affairs. To each according to his apparent need, the uncle had offered aid, and from each had taken a note of hand for the amount loaned—a proceeding at which each nephew smiled to himself, reflecting that the force of habit was strong with Uncle Pierre, and that while the old man's purpose was obvious, his characteristic secretiveness would not permit him to state it clearly. This conclusion on the part of each nephew that *he* was the favorite nephew and prospective heir, was emphasized and made certain by the request which old Pierre made of each that he should say nothing to any of the others concerning the manner in which he had been favored.

Each of the nephews had been advised by their uncle to use this money carefully. Each observed the avuncular injunction according to his personal idiosyncracy. Adolphe Beaurepas paid off the mortgage on his plantation, which amounted to ten thousand dollars, but, instead of holding the remaining five thousand in reserve against future contingencies, embarked in another speculation, which proved a failure and left him merely square with the world, except for the debt to his uncle, which caused him no uneasiness. He was not a married man—none of the nephews were married. That their uncle meant his heir to marry Josephine Morales was known to them all, a plan which could not be carried out unless the heir was an unmarried man. Naturally of a secretive, mole-like disposition, it was no trouble for Adolphe to observe his uncle's wish and keep his own counsel, which he did, and dreamed of future opulence.

Hector Beaurepas paid off the more pressing of his debts, and immediately began to contract large additional obligations. Raoul made good his speculations. Henri bought his mistress a new wardrobe, and spent the rest at roulette in a certain gambling den on Canal Street, backing a system which he had figured out to a mathematical certainty would break the bank. But, apart from any resultant evidences of prosperity, there was a general increase among the nephews of pride and self-importance, which had it been confined to any single one of them, would have been quite noticeable to the others. That they did not observe it was due to the fact that each of them had shifted his own position to the same viewpoint. It was, of course, perfectly natural that their scale of living and expenditure should increase. The prospective heir of the wealthiest man in New Orleans must live on a scale commensurate with his expectations. Each Beaurepas, therefore, wondered at the extravagance of the others, and deplored with complacent sadness the ultimate certainty of their disappointment; nor, because of the promise made to their uncle, could he warn them against the consequences of a prodigality which their uncle's intention would not justify.

Meantime, old Pierre Beaurepas clung tenaciously though feebly to life. He had lived through three-quarters of the hundred years that made up the life of the city. He had seen it bandied from nation to nation—from France to Spain, from Spain to France, from France to the United States. He had seen it grow from a small provincial settlement in a fever-ridden marsh until it was obviously destined to become one of the greatest cities of the continent. For more than forty years he had been a power in the commercial and social life of the city, and he wished to carry on as long as he might. To live might demand a struggle, but—*le jeu valait la chandelle*—the prize was worth the effort. He maintained a healthy interest in business and went down once or twice a month to his office in the Bank of New Orleans, of which he was the largest stockholder and a director. Meantime his heir might wait—the inheritance was well worth waiting for. He had his books—Rabelais, Molière, Racine, Rousseau, Voltaire,

Montesquieu—the master minds of their country's literature. His collection of French memoirs was the finest in America, as were his French and Spanish paintings. A Velasquez which belonged to him is now in the Metropolitan Museum of Art, the gift of a millionaire who bought it for a round sum in a later generation. Everything that could conduce to physical and intellectual comfort in his declining years was at his command. If there was something he missed, if he had any secret regret or sorrow, and who has not, it was shared by no one, and he kept it locked in his own bosom.

CHAPTER IV

—————➤●◄—————

Philippe and Josephine

PHILIPPE BEAUREPAS was singing, light-heartedly, sna-
tches from a Creole love song, as he rode along the
avenue of mighty trees, draped with Spanish moss,
which lined the Natchez Road from the city to Trois
Pigeons plantation. To the left at a little distance and
visible through the trees, lay the broad river, and to the
right plantations of cotton and cane, with now and
then a large plantation house with the slave quarters
grouped around or near it, and dark-hued laborers
toiling with plow or hoe. Philippe was astride of a good
horse, the road was dry, the morning fair, there was an
aromatic breeze from over the river and all nature was
in tune with his mood, and as he rode he sang:

> "'Delaide, mo la reine,
> Chimin-la trop longue pour alle,
> Chimin-la monte dans le hauts,
> Tout piti qui mo ye,

M'alle monte la haut dans courant,
C'est moin, Liron, qui rive
M'alle di ye
Bon soir, mo la reine
C'est moin, Liron, qui rive."

" 'Delaide, my queen, the way is long,
That leads upstream to thee,
But, though I'm small, the current strong
Will be as naught to me.
'Tis I, Liron, who come,
I come to thee,
Good night, my queen!
'Tis I, Liron, who come."[1]

At Trois Pigeons dwelt Don José Morales, in the large, sprawling, substantially built in the Spanish fashion, but now somewhat dilapidated frame house erected by his father fifty years before. It was neither the house, however, nor old Don José that drew Philippe Beaurepas toward Trois Pigeons. The magnet which attracted him was none other than Josephine, Don José's seventeen-year-old daughter, born when he was past fifty, cherished by him as the apple of his eye and also as his chief bulwark against ever encroaching bankruptcy.

Don José Morales was the bosom friend of old Pierre Beaurepas. It was not, upon the surface, a well-assorted friendship. Pierre Beaurepas, as we have seen, was the wealthiest man in New Orleans. Don José, in spite of his ancient name and Spanish pride, was known to be

in perennial hard luck. The plantation had been mortgaged for two generations. From whatever defect of
skill or ability, Don José usually failed where others
succeeded. If his next door neighbor made a good crop
of indigo, the Morales growth would either prove a failure in the field or be spoiled in the manufacture. When
other planters changed to cane and began to boil sugar,
Don José clung to indigo. If he speculated in cotton he
was always caught on the losing side of the market. His
slaves bred poorly and were subject to epidemics that
carried them off like sick cattle. They even took the
yellow fever, to which most blacks were immune. One
year the sugar-house had been burned; another year a
crevasse in the levee had inundated the plantation.

Pierre Beaurepas held the mortgage on Trois Pigeons, in spite of which the friendship remained un-
broken, a most remarkable circumstance when the
deadly effect of debt on friendship is borne in mind.
Who avoids one so much as he who owes him five
dollars or ten? If so small a sum can have so potent an
influence, what must be said of a friendship which can
survive the consciousness, upon the one hand, that
one's debtor is embarrassed and one's security doubt-
ful, and upon the other, that one is at the mercy of his
creditors?

The most essential element of friendship is equality.
That this particular friendship should survive under
these conditions, was due to the fact that it was rooted
in matters more vital than those which dealt with gold.

Even the most sentimental of Creoles would have smiled at the suggestion that to José Morales, always in debt, or to Pierre Beaurepas, landlord and money-lender, anything could be more important than gold. And yet there was a romance in their lives. Years before, when both were young, they had been comrades in an expedition against the pirates who from time to time, during a period of years, infested the lower Mississippi. In an encounter with these miscreants, José Morales had interposed his own body to receive the stroke of a cutlass aimed at the head of Pierre Beaurepas, who lay stunned and senseless upon the deck of the good ship *Bon Espoir*. Pierre Beaurepas had always remembered the obligation and never considered the debt as paid. It was the one sentimental episode, except his marriage, so far as anyone knew, that had marked the career of this keenest of New Orleans businessmen. If there had been another, as may appear, it had not been for the public.

For many years the two men, living in the same city neighborhood, had seen one another almost daily. When Don José had given up his town house and gone to live entirely on his plantation, and Pierre's health had begun to fail, they still exchanged visits at least once a month. They were both expert chess players, and if the game were not completed at the end of a meeting, the positions would be noted and the contest resumed when next they came together. If Morales were ever unable to pay the interest on the mortgage, his friend merely charged it against him on the ledger. Neither of them seemed to worry about the future.

"My heir," said Pierre, "shall marry your daughter. The mortgage will thus merge into the estate."

"She shall marry no other man, I swear," Morales was wont to answer.

When Josephine was twelve years old she gave promise of unusual beauty.

"My heir will be a very fortunate man," said old Pierre one day to his friend, glancing at the maid with rare appreciation.

"Which of your nephews is to be the heir?" Morales asked, removing his long black cigar from his lips. "The girl is approaching womanhood, and it would be well to guide her fancy in the right direction. You have several handsome nephews."

"Tell her, José, to keep her heart free! But she is still a child, and perhaps it would be better to tell her nothing. I have not yet named my heir."

Josephine was a pupil of the Ursuline Convent. Had she been kept always under lock and key, perhaps her heart might have remained entirely free. But her mother was dead, and her father not inordinately strict. She had many opportunities to meet young people, especially the Beaurepas cousins. They had played together as children, before Señor Morales had sold his town house and taken up his residence at Trois Pigeons. She had always thought Philippe the handsomest of the lot, and Philippe, while yet a lad, had perceived, with the temperamental precociousness of the subtropics, that Josephine was beautiful. More than once he had told her so.

"Josephine," he would say, "you are the most beautiful of women. I love you and wish more than anything else in the world to marry you."

"Hush, Philippe," she had replied, "you must not say such things to me. My father has promised your uncle that I shall marry his heir."

"And why may I not be the heir?" demanded Philippe, stoutly. Until Josephine raised it, the question of the inheritance had never been considered very seriously by Philippe. It was a pleasing possibility but he had not built upon it. He had been bred a gentleman, had been educated, clothed and nurtured as a gentleman, and expected by his own exertions to be able to live as a gentleman. He had no expensive vices—he was neither drunkard, nor gambler, nor roué. But after Josephine had spoken thus, the inheritance assumed an added value in his eyes. To be his uncle's heir was to marry Josephine; not to be the heir might mean to lose her, not necessarily, but the probabilities were that way.

It was not a situation to bring out the best that was in a man. Such a rivalry with one's own relations is apt to develop the sneak, the time-server, the hypocrite. One must seek to please at the cost of inclination, thus breeding insincerity, and sometimes hatred where one must seem to love; for nature does not like to be forced, and has a way of striking balances. There was once a slave who kept in a secret place an effigy of his master, upon which he returned with interest and satisfaction all the kicks and cuffs his master had bestowed upon him. An old voodoo woman had told him that his master would feel them all.

Philippe had preserved, under temptation, a fine integrity. Desiring above all things to marry Josephine, he sought to be worthy of her. And if, for the same reason, he tried to please his uncle, it was no effort, because he acknowledged a debt of gratitude to him for many things.

"I owe him all I am and all I have," he said to himself, with simple loyalty. "He is my uncle and the head of our family, and I could do no less than love him."

He felt sure that his uncle appreciated his devotion, which was in marked contrast to the obsequious sycophancy of several of the other nephews. He was not energetic, Philippe was not; he could perhaps keep what he had, but was not likely to add to it greatly by his own exertions. He would make an ideal heir for a rich man.

Josephine had kept him at arm's length for a long time.

"You should love me, Josephine," he would say, "as I love you."

"But imagine," she would reply, "that you should not

be the heir, in what a predicament I should be placed! Loving you, I should be compelled to wed another. You would not wish me such a fate?"

No, he would not. He could not think of Josephine as another's, without a shudder.

"Perish the thought!" he cried. "I should run away with you."

"No, Philippe, you could not. The church would not approve."

"I would marry you *à l'américain*, before a magistrate."

"No, Philippe, I could not marry without the blessing of the church, nor without my father's consent."

Don José did nothing to interfere with their friendship. He thought of it as nothing more than a childish fancy which would yield to the serious exigencies of life. Moreover, Philippe might be the heir—his friend Pierre had always spoken kindly of Philippe. Again, Philippe had no entanglements of the heart to interfere with Josephine's happiness. If he should be the heir, he might take Josephine with her father's blessing. If not, she would do her duty. She was too desirable for any but the best; and there were other reasons, powerful ones, which must constrain her.

Philippe thought he had good grounds for his elation as he rode along the way to Trois Pigeons. Only the day before, his uncle had sent for him and had asked for an estimate of his debts. He was, by the way, a real estate broker and dealer.

"I do not owe a picayune which is not amply se-

cured, Uncle Pierre," he had answered, "except my tai-
lor's bill, and that can wait."

His uncle had seemed surprised.

"Your business would pay better with more capital
invested," he said, "I will lend you twenty thousand
dollars. Put it in houses. The city is growing. In two
years you will have doubled it. You may give me your
note for the money. But say nothing to the others about
it. You are the only one that deserves it."

Philippe had accepted the proffered loan, regarding
it and his uncle's commendation, as an earnest of his
heirship; and he was now on his way to Trois Pigeons
with joy in his heart and a song upon his lips, to impart
his momentous secret to Josephine.

AS Philippe drew near enough to see the belvedere of
Trois Pigeons rising above the treetops, he came face to
face with a strange cavalcade. Not so strange either,
indeed, but striking. A giant, deeply pockmarked
Negro and a one-eyed mulatto, shackled together,
wrist to wrist and ankle to ankle, so that they must move
as one man, were stumbling along the road, and behind
them came, on horseback, a white man by courtesy,
long of hair, swarthy of skin, high of cheek bone, with
a huge sombrero on his head, a pistol at his belt, and in
his hand a rawhide whip. It was Mendoza, the half-
breed Spanish Indian overseer of Don José Morales.

"Good day, Monsieur Beaurepas," said the overseer
with a wave of the hand.

"Good day, Mendoza. Who are these scurvy rascals?"

"Hist! Monsieur Philippe, say nothing at the house. They are masterless men—runaways. I found them on the plantation. Señor Morales ordered them whipped, and then would have let them go."

"We are free men," protested the mulatto. "Our boat was overturned in the river and we sought refuge on the bank. One would not treat a dog so."

"Silence, brute," said the overseer, with a slash of the whip which left an angry welt across the speaker's face. "They have no free papers," he went on. "My salary is a year behind. I shall turn them over to the authorities. If they cannot prove their freedom, they will be sold as vagrants and my share of the money will pay me up."

It was a lawful thing. Runaway slaves were danger-ous to society. A Negro without proof of his freedom was presumed to be a runaway slave. Philippe glanced at the two manacled men. They were desperate looking fellows, the mulatto seeming even fiercer than the black, as he glowered at the two white men with his one menacing eye, like a chained tiger.

"Ah, well, Mendoza, I wish you good luck. It is well you have them shackled, or they would murder you before you reached the city."

"Never fear, Monsieur Philippe. It is my trade to manage such cattle. You will find the señora at home."

Philippe rode on until he entered the gate of Trois Pigeons, and dismounted in the patio. A Negro lad sprang forward and took charge of his horse. A colored girl standing on the verandah darted into the house to warn her mistress. The house servants all loved their young mistress and took a personal interest in her love affair, with the conditional character of which they were all familiar.

As Philippe set foot upon the verandah, Josephine came forward to meet him—a Southern beauty, moving with an unconscious, undulatory grace. Her gown of dotted white muslin was made in the Empire style, low in the neck, with short sleeves, clearly defining, above the high waistline, the youthful curve of her well-formed bosom. She wore this free costume with virginal modesty, though her arms were bare, and her somewhat worn red morocco mules nursed the soft white skin of her little feet with no jealous stocking to intervene. Of the pure Spanish type, she might have stepped direct from a Goya canvas. The broad low brow of her little head was crowned with a wealth of dark hair, which she had washed that morning, and which, gathered loosely with a red ribbon, fell in a dusky flood far below her waist.

From the clear olive of her face, to which the excitement of Philippe's visit had lent a dash of a richer color, her large dark eyes, shaded by long lashes over which her arched eyebrows nearly met, flashed welcome to her lover as she held forth a hand which showed, as clearly as a human hand could show, that none of her ancestors had ever done any work.

"Welcome, Philippe," she said, with shy warmth.

"Good day, Josephine. Is your father at home?"

"No, Philippe, he is at the far end of the plantation. Will you ride out to him?"

"No, Josephine, I will wait."

"Shall I send a Negro for him?"

"No, Josephine. I would not disturb him. It is you I came to see."

Josephine sighed a sigh of contentment. They went into the cool high-ceilinged hall. They were alone except for the servants about the house. Her duenna, an elderly cousin of her father who made her home with them, was taking her siesta in the adjoining room, but she was a hard sleeper. Philippe told Josephine of his uncle's generosity, and of his own convictions.

"Is it not clear, Josephine, that I shall be the heir?"

"There can be no doubt of it, Philippe. You are the best of them all, and your uncle has perceived it, and has chosen this way to indicate his preference. He does not make his choice known to the others, because he is an old man, and he would end his days in peace."

"Then, Josephine," cried Philippe, "there is no reason you should not love me."

"N-o, Philippe, I suppose—"

But she had not time to finish, for he closed her lips with a kiss. They were seated side by side on the faded Louis Quinze settee. He was reaching for another kiss, when a sudden barking of dogs and scurrying of Negro children in the yard, announced an important arrival.

"It is papa," said Josephine, starting to her feet. "I'll go and meet him."

Old Don José shook hands with Philippe. He listened with a grave interest to Philippe's story.

"It is a good sign," he said. "You have substantial ground for hope. How is he?"

"Feeble in health, but bright and keen in mind. Since there is no doubt, Señor Morales, there can be no objection to my coming oftener?"

"Patience, Philippe, patience! He has not named the heir—the cup has not yet reached the lip. Josephine is young and must not be bound by a betrothal, nor would I have her affections too deeply involved. When my friend Pierre announces that you are to be his heir, you may have her with my blessing. Until then, you may see her once a month, Philippe, once a month. Wait and hope!"

Philippe went away disconsolate. Once a month! Well, he would see her oftener than that!

She came to town now and then to hear mass or to shop, in company with her duenna or a servant, and he would set a Negro lad to watch the Natchez Road and notify him whenever Mademoiselle Morales came to town.

CHAPTER V

———➤●◄———

The Quadroon Ball

THOUGH LOUISIANA had been part of the American Republic for nearly twenty years, the historic visit of a French duke to New Orleans, which took place at about this period, was an event of tremendous social importance. The spiritual nexus which bound the Creoles to the land of their forefathers had been modified but not destroyed by the change of political dominion. The echoes of the French Revolution still resounded loudly in New Orleans, although its watchword of "Liberty, Equality and Fraternity" no more harmonized with slavery and the Code Noir than did the Declaration of Independence, and the fall of the Bastille still continued to be celebrated.

As a matter of fact, Louisiana had never been a free commonwealth until 1808, when it became a state of the Union. The bureaucratic monarchy of Louis Quinze, which from a distance of four thousand miles regulated every petty detail of government, had been succeeded by a Spanish despotism really less meddlesome, but seemingly more oppressive because of the lack of sympathy between rulers and ruled. Upon its formal return to France in 1803, the colony had been sold by Napoleon, without consulting the inhabitants, for a ridiculously small sum, to the United States, and the political status of the former province became and continued to be for several years after the American annexation that of a territory. The only spark of independence in the history of the city had been the futile resistance made to the transfer of the colony to Spain in 1768, and this momentary self-assertion had been so severely punished that it was never repeated. The American occupation had been received with protests loud and deep, but without active hostility. French by blood and temperament, and for thirty years the sole remnant of the French colonies in North America, Louisiana—for as Paris was France, so New Orleans was Louisiana—clung tenaciously to the language of France—of Bienville and Frontenac, of all the pioneers who had covered the history of New France with glory—and held fast to the Catholic faith and to the traditions of the mother country. Reflecting, sentimentally, the political movements of France, the Creoles had shared the glory of Napoleon, and though no longer French politically, had cheered the restoration of the monarchy. So that, even as late as 1820, the visit of a royal duke of the restored dynasty was something more than a social event; it struck a slumbering chord of loyalty to race and caste, which neither conquest nor purchase had destroyed.

New Orleans, therefore, had exerted itself to entertain fittingly the Duc de Nemours.[1] There were dinners, *fêtes* and balls galore; there were discreet *petits soupers* and *parties carrées*; for the duke was a gay young blade and French to the core; some years of exile in England had been only partly compensated by a very lively career after the restoration. A desire to see the world, as well as the wish to escape from an embarrassing entanglement, had brought his royal highness to America and to New Orleans. As a stranger, the duke was interested in objects of local interest, and was introduced to all the pleasures of the town. The lottery held a special drawing during his visit. The gaming houses on Canal and Carondelet Streets, upon which his highness looked in now and then, were much frequented by those who wished to see a duke play at cards or roulette. There was an extra season of opera, a grand ball for the social elite of the city, and on another night of the same week, a quadroon ball of unparalleled splendor.

This institution, for many years a feature of New Orleans life, was an outgrowth of the exotic civilization of a pioneer race, who, bringing with them no wives, before the advent of women of their own race, had mated, more or less like the birds, with the Indian and Negro women. Though frequently severe and even cruel slaveholders, the Latins have nevertheless always shown a marked affinity for the darker races, for whom they had never the harsh Anglo-Saxon contempt. Recognizing their own blood, too, even when mingled with that of slaves, it had always been the fashion in Latin America to manumit the children of these left-handed unions, and to provide for their support. There had thus grown up in New Orleans the large class of free colored people known as the quadroon caste, of which Paul and Julie Marchand were members, the women of which, say the chroniclers of those days, vied with the white Creole women in beauty, in dress, and in graceful dancing. And the quadroon women were the reason for the quadroon ball.

The quadroon ball was held on Thursday night, following the grand ball on Wednesday night. The presence of a royal duke was as exciting an event to the frail tinted beauties of the French quarter as to the paler ladies of the aristocracy. Every staid quadroon, long since retired upon a legacy or a pension, wished to be present; every young girl with a future yet to be provided for, fluttered with excitement at the prospect of meeting, in a scene of brilliant gaiety, a royal duke of France. Their life—poor butterflies of passion, poor hostages for the chastity of their white sisters—their life yet had its compensations. They gained freedom, ease, sometimes a love, which, whatever it may have lacked of the romantic devotion which goes by that name, preserved them from the pains of poverty and brought to their children beauty and brains and sometimes wealth. It brought, too, the quadroon ball, boxes at the opera, a veneer of courtesy, under which lurked, of course, the brutality inseparable from slavery and all its incidents, but it spread a fair covering of flowers over the morass, and one might, if one chose, shut one's eyes to the spot where the cloak was thin or the slough laid bare.

The quadroon ball was, of course, for white gentlemen only. No amount of wealth or education could qualify a male quadroon for this gathering of the cream of his own womanhood. They were meat for his masters. Meekness and self-effacement were the price which the quadroon man paid for the privilege of living and doing business in New Orleans. If he could find a wife among the younger quadroon women, all well and good, but if she were personally attractive he did well to keep her in seclusion. If he were not so fortunate, he might hire or buy a black or colored housekeeper, or perhaps marry the endowed mistress of some white man who had tired of her when her cheeks began to fade or her eyes to lose their luster. For the wealthier quadroons were themselves sometimes the owners of slaves. With most of them the love of liberty, like that of their betters, was mainly personal. If they chafed under the existing system, it was less from any abstract love of freedom than because of their own restrictions. They would have loved, for instance, to frequent the fashionable gaming houses or attend the quadroon balls; now and then one of them who could not be casually distinguished from white would try it, at the imminent risk of recognitions and consequent ignominious expulsion.

On the evening of the quadroon ball in honor of the Duc de Nemours, Paul Marchand, arriving home late from his office, found his wife in the living room of the house on Bourbon Street where they lived. The children had been put to bed, and through the door leading into the adjoining dining room he could see the table set for his dinner and catch the appetizing odor of food cooked as only a Creole cook could prepare it. He had a healthy appetite, but this did not prevent him from seeing that his wife was preoccupied and ill at ease.

"What is the matter, Julie?" he demanded. "What is it that deranges you?"

"I am alarmed about Lizette. She has been out since three o'clock. I did not wish her to go alone, and Cuffy accompanied her. I expected her back at six. I sent Cuffy back for her at half after seven, but the house was closed and his knock brought no response."

"Where did she go from here?"

"To Madame Claudine's, to try on her new gown."

"Where can she be?"

"I suspect, Paul, that she has gone —"

"Where?"

"To the Salle Condé." The quadroon balls took place in a hall on Condé Street.

Paul Marchand's face flushed darkly. His wife, de-

spite her origin, had been carefully reared and educated. He had married her before she had scarcely
come into contact with the outer world. Her sister Lizette had been as carefully brought up, but a touch of
waywardness had made her chafe under conventional
restraints. Vain, frivolous, beautiful in the quadroon
way, the blood of the gay Creole gentlemen and their
dusky sweethearts throbbed in her veins in a ceaseless
demand for excitement, gaiety, pleasure. Marchand
had planned to take her with his wife and children to
France, and there, with the money her father had left
her, to marry her to some gentleman to whom, with
Gallic liberality, the bar sinister and the dash of African
blood would not outweigh an ample dowry. If, however, there should be any added disability to overcome,
the task would be by that much the more difficult.
Even the most liberal of decent Frenchmen was likely
to demand the elementary virtue in a wife. For an unmarried young woman to attend the quadroon ball
was, to all intents and purposes, by the social code of
New Orleans, a bid for the protection, without the
marriage ceremony, of some gentleman who could afford such a luxury. Paris was not so far from New Orleans but that many people of the latter city, both white
and colored, were often in the French capital. While a
student there Marchand had formed a wide acquaintance among the younger men of the city. He had met,
in one or two gay parties, this very duke whose visit
was the occasion of this very ball; the duke had per-

haps forgotten him, nor would he wish to recall himself to his remembrance. In Paris they had met upon the sort of equality upon which gentlemen everywhere meet in public places. He had even engaged in a fencing bout with his highness once, in a Parisian *salle d'armes* where Marchand was conspicuous for his skill with the foils. If they should meet in New Orleans it would have to be on a very different footing, and he therefore preferred that they should not meet at all. Lizette at the ball, with her very striking beauty, would be sure to attract attention, with the attendant advertisement, and the consequent reflection upon his own family.

"She has been very restless and excited," said Julie. "She has wondered what a royal duke was like, and was telling me only today of Madame Claudine's entrancing description of the quadroon balls. I fear, Paul, that she has gone there."

"Let me see," said Paul, "the ball begins at eight. I shall go at once and fetch her home."

"You'll not be admitted," said his wife.

"It's a masked ball," replied Paul. "I'll wear a domino. If I can but get her ear, I shall bring her away. She will hardly have arrived."

"You'll run the risk of insult if you go."

"We shall run the risk of dishonor if I don't."

Julie, after a brief search, found a black domino, or half-mask, and Marchand, having thrust it into his pocket, hastened down Carondelet Street to the corner of Condé and soon reached the building, later occupied by a convent of colored nuns, but in this earlier generation devoted to scenes of pleasure in which the quadroon and octoroon women of that age played anything but a conventual role. The front was brilliantly lighted. As Marchand approached, a lemon-tinted, deep-bosomed young woman, in an elaborate ball gown, satin slippers, a light wrap thrown across her bare shoulders, was entering the hall on the arm of the son of the mayor of New Orleans. Marchand stood for a moment and watched them pass through the lighted portal, in which stood a very tall mulatto in gorgeous livery—black men were not allowed at the quadroon balls in any capacity, under pain of death, though they might light the way of women thither with lanterns. It was a small city, and carriages were seldom used in going to balls of any kind.

As Marchand, having put on his mask approached the door and was about to enter it, the porter, touching his cap respectfully, barred the way.

"Pardon, miché, but your ticket?"

Marchand ran his hands through his pockets as though searching for his ticket, but of course found nothing, since he had no ticket.

"I've evidently left it behind," he replied, with an air of annoyance.

"Then your name, miché, if you please?"

Marchand hesitated, but for a moment only. Slipping his hand into his pocket, he drew forth a gold piece which he slipped into the doorman's hand.

"I wish to preserve my incognito," he murmured. "It is all right; I belong to the duke's suite."

The doorkeeper in turn hesitated, but the bribe was a large one, and the visitor was undoubtedly a gentleman.

"Enter miché, and a thousand thanks for your generosity. Miché le Duc is just ahead of you."

Marchand mounted the stairs hastily. He had dressed himself before leaving home, in the costume of the period, which was a copy, not more than a year behind, of that of the Paris court and salon. The elegance of his attire, the clear olive of his complexion, so far as it was visible around the small black mask, in contrast with the straight, brown hair which fell to his shoulders; his slender but sinewy hand, with the nails carefully trimmed and polished and bearing several rings set with precious stones, made up a *tout ensemble* which no one would have suspected as belonging to other than a gentleman of the first social rank. Absorbed in his quest and protected from recognition by his mask, Marchand moved freely among the gathering throng.

The scene was a brilliant one. The large ballroom, profusely decorated with cut flowers and potted palms, was lighted by a grand chandelier with dozens of wax candles and crystal pendants shivering with the vibration of the dance, and flashing with all the colors of the spectrum. The floor was of solid oak, three inches thick, said to be the best dancing floor in New Orleans. Most of the women were young and shapely, many of them not casually distinguishable from white, and the men, also for the most part young, were of the cream of New Orleans society. A mulatto orchestra was playing Gottschalk's *Danse Nègre*,[2] replete with the languorous tropical charm of Creole melody. The ball was not yet in full swing, but a few couples were moving over the polished floor to the rhythm of the music.

Marchand threw a hasty glance around the ballroom but did not discover the object of his search. But in one corner, in vivacious conversation with a well-known merchant with whom he himself had dealings, he recognized under her mask, the sprightly Madame Claudine, the fashionable quadroon *modiste* of the Rue Carondelet, the full battery of whose sparkling eyes and full-blown charms, set off by one of the famous gowns of her own make with which she clothed the *élégantes* of New Orleans, was in active operation. Costly diamonds sparkled in her ears, and she toyed with a fan which had belonged to Marie Antoinette. For Claudine was rich and went every two years to Paris to bring back the latest fashions. It was the dream of her life to live in that city and conduct a pension for colonial gentlemen.

Marchand started toward her and had covered more than half the distance between them, when he hesitated. That Lizette was at the ball he had no doubt, but was it desirable for him to make his presence known to Madame Claudine? It was not at all necessary for her to know that he had attended the quadroon ball—it was a serious breach of caste, which if known, could do him no good. If Claudine should be indiscreet enough to mention it afterwards, it might still further complicate a situation which he was beginning to find well-nigh intolerable.

Through the long French windows he could see the couples promenading in the broad gallery which ran alongside the ballroom, where a dance may be set out or whispered flirtation carried on. Marchand moved toward the nearest window. It was necessary, in order to reach it, to pass a group of gentlemen who stood engaged in animated conversation. In one of these Marchand recognized the young duke, who, as the guest of the evening, was unmasked, and he recognized, with the keen memory of hatred, the voice of the gentleman who was addressing the duke.

"We shall unmask in ten minutes. It is unfair to deprive your highness any longer of the full splendor of these charms. I will give the signal at nine o'clock on the minute; those who come in costume will have arrived by that hour—if not, it is their own fault."

"I saw just now," returned the duke, "a girl who struck my fancy. She was gowned in pale yellow and had the figure of a Hebe in miniature. I shall be glad to see her face, I'm sure it will be in keeping. There she goes now," he added, nodding toward the opposite side of the room.

Marchand's eyes followed those of the duke, and rested upon Lizette, who was at that moment entering the room by another door. She was masked, but he could not have mistaken her anywhere. He had seen the stuff of which her gown was made; he himself had made her a Christmas present of the necklace she wore, and she walked with a seductive grace that bordered unconsciously upon wantonness.

"I'll introduce your highness as soon as we unmask," said Henri Beaurepas, whom Marchand had recognized in the speaker. "Perhaps we need not wait. She is at present unattended, and you may not be allowed a monopoly after she unmasks. She will likely prove a pleasant acquaintance and worth following up. I have designs of my own in that quarter, but will yield precedence to a distinguished guest—whose visit is a short one!" he concluded with a significant laugh.

Marchand darted before them and moved swiftly through the crowd toward Lizette. He wished by all means to prevent her unmasking at this ball. He expected to sail for France in a few weeks and take the girl with him. In a country where their origin entailed no insurmountable social disabilities, and with means and education which would gain them admission to good social circles, it was not at all unlikely that the Duc de Nemours, an aristocrat with democratic tastes, might come face to face in some Paris ballroom with

Lizette. The manners and morals of Europe were none too strict a century ago, but respectable women did not attend the students' balls in the Latin Quarter nor the more brilliant assemblies of the demimonde, to which the quadroon balls of New Orleans could only be compared. It was important, therefore, that Marchand should reach his sister-in-law and get her away from the ball unnoticed before the moment for unmasking.

His movements, however, had not been unobserved. Henri Beaurepas had noticed the start with which the man in the black domino had paused beside his own group and had observed the rapid movement of Marchand toward the corner where Lizette was seated. Excusing himself for a moment, he left the duke in conversation with the third member of his party and followed Marchand quickly across the room, in time to hear him address the young woman.

"Lizette," he said sternly, "you must come away immediately. You should not be here. The signal for unmasking will be given in three minutes. If you're not away by then, your good name will be ruined and our family disgraced."

Lizette had started guiltily. She knew she was in the wrong and did not stop to argue.

"I'll get my cloak," she said, rising at once and moving toward the cloakroom.

Henri Beaurepas had overheard the colloquy and had recognized the speaker. Quadroon men were not allowed at the *cordon bleu* balls. This intruder had broken caste. A man of finer fiber might have recognized the provocation and have helped rather than hindered a praiseworthy action. But Henri Beaurepas was not a man of fine fiber. Not only had he promised the duke an introduction to this tropical butterfly, but beneath her mask he had recognized the young girl who only a few days before had cast him a most coquettish glance from Claudine's front window in Carondelet Street. This was a golden opportunity, which he by no means wished to forfeit. He would like, too, to punish the insolence of this quadroon, who had more than once, in other places, assumed to exercise the privileges of white gentlemen. There must be some way to get rid of him, and at the same time prevent scandal which might mar the harmony of the occasion.

"I have it," he said to himself with a gesture of satisfaction. Turning to the dancers behind him, he touched one and then another upon the shoulder, and in a moment had a little group of four or five young men around him, among them his brother Hector. He whispered to them certain instructions, and they moved off toward the entrance.

Meantime Lizette had donned her cloak and come toward Marchand, who tendered his arm and started toward the doorway. As they approached the main entrance a liveried servant came forward and said in Negro French: "If monsieur will permit me, gentlemen and ladies wishing to leave the ballroom can pass out unobserved by the side entrance."

He motioned toward a door at the side. As they approached it, several gentlemen converged upon them as if by accident, Marchand was separated from Lizette, and a moment later found himself upon the other side of the door, which was closed between them. At the same moment his arm was grasped upon either side. As, taken utterly by surprise, he struggled to free himself and struck out with blind indignation, he suffered some violence in return and received a blow upon the head which stretched him senseless on the pavement.

CHAPTER VI

———⟫●⟪———

In the Calabozo

WHEN MARCHAND recovered consciousness he found himself lying on a rough bed in the Calabozo, or city prison. What hour of the night it was he did not know, for the prison was shrouded in darkness, except for the dim light of a lantern which but faintly illuminated the corridor, so that he was unable to consult his watch.

The quadroon men were, as a rule, of amiable disposition and cheerful temperament. While they regarded their social treatment as cruel and unjust, and discussed it among themselves with much animation, the cruelty was mainly a matter of feeling and might be ignored by the philosophical; and to the injustice, consisting for the most part of things denied instead of things taken away, they were at least accustomed, with the callousness which custom engenders. While regarded as inferior to the whites, they were looked upon and treated as much superior to the darker people.

One of the principal streets of the city was named after a free woman of color, who owned the land through which it was opened. This discrimination in their favor was also, to one not a philosopher, a source of comfort. Whether or not the Creole quadroons were a philosophic race was not really important, since the pleasure-loving French temperament, superimposed upon the easygoing African, produced a usually placid acceptance of the situation which had all the effect of philosophy.

In this respect, however, Paul Marchand differed from the average quadroon. Whether it was the fiery spirit of some adventurous European ancestor, or the blood of some African chief who had exercised the power of life and death before being broken to the hoe, or whether the free air of revolutionary France had wrought upon him—whatever the reason, he had chafed more than most under the restriction of his caste.

When the restraints and humiliations to which he was subjected had culminated in his rude arrest and ruder imprisonment, is it to be wondered that his bosom was filled with stormy feelings which found a poor vent in pacing up and down the narrow cell, and impotent shaking of his fists and trilling the r's of picturesque French oaths? For despite any reputed strain of alien blood, Paul Marchand was French to the finger tips; no Creole of Louisiana was truer to type.

When he had worked off his first paroxysm of rage,

he began to consider his predicament. It was a matter for serious thought. His position was an awkward one. In the altercation at the ballroom he had struck several white men, among them Hector Beaurepas. Under the Code Noir, for a man of color to strike a white man was to render himself liable, before the law, if he escaped immediate death at the hands of the person struck, to fine, imprisonment, whipping, or, in an aggravated case, the loss of the hand which had struck the blow. Obviously he would need a good lawyer, and it would be well to summon him at once. He ought also to send a message to his wife, apprising her of his whereabouts.

Marchand raised his voice and called for a jailer. There was no response. He called again more loudly and shook the iron bars of the cell door. There was still no response, but from the adjoining cell came a Spanish oath, and a gruff voice, demanding, in Gumbo French, why he was making such an infernal racket in the middle of the night, when honest and respectable prisoners were trying to sleep. Finding it impossible to secure the attention of a jailer, Marchand made the best of the situation, composed himself upon the layer of foul straw spread on the floor in lieu of a bed, and joined the ranks of the honest and peaceable prisoners who sought forgetfulness of their troubles in slumber.

He had slept he did not know how long, when gradually there stole upon his senses the sounds of a whispered conversation, and as he slowly returned to consciousness he discovered that these sounds came from the cell adjoining his own. Whether the mortar had fallen out from between the stones of the old partition wall, or whether, in the stillness of midnight, his ear was attuned to just the pitch that would catch, through the barred front of his own cell, the whispered words which sounded from the one adjoining, in any event the conversation was distinctly audible.

"It is an outrage," said an unctuous Negro voice. "We have done nothing; they had no means of knowing that we intended to do anything. We were beaten without mercy; we were thrown into prison; we are to be sold into slavery, because, forsooth, we cannot prove that we are free men!"

"We shall have revenge," returned a harsher voice, which to Marchand sounded vaguely familiar. "I hate them all, root and branch. I would kill the last one, even as our people did in San Domingo. Yet it is a large contract, and we might ourselves be killed in the process."

"True," replied the other, "but we need not attempt so much. They have all injured us, but not all equally. If we can avenge ourselves upon those who whipped us and sent us here, it would be at least something on account."

The conversation proceeded for a quarter of an hour. Once a rat scurrying across the floor from some unoccupied cell caused them to be silent for a few minutes. Reassured that they were not being overheard, they resumed their conversation, which took the form of a plot to burn down a certain plantation house, west of the city, to cut the levee and flood the plantation, and to poison the cattle and horses in the stables.

Marchand listened with instinctive interest. Himself the proprietor, through his wife, of several houses and a plantation, the destruction of property appealed to him as to any other landowner. He listened intently and finally gathered from their description of it, that the place marked for destruction was the house of old Don José Morales, five miles from the city, along the Natchez Road.

Negro insurrections were ever the nightmare of slavery. They rarely occurred, but were always feared—conscience makes cowards of us all. Under the strict repressive discipline of the pioneer French and Spanish slaveholders, such few risings as had ever been attempted, were small and easily suppressed, and the single one which took place in Louisiana after the American occupation, had proved a costly failure for the rioters. Nevertheless, the awful example of San Domingo, where the land, for its sins, had been drenched in blood, was always before the eyes of those just across the Gulf of Mexico who still fostered the institution of slavery.

Under other circumstances Marchand would have been deeply impressed and indeed shocked by this conversation, and would have felt it his duty to warn the authorities and denounce the conspirators. But his recent experiences had drawn him for the moment away from his quadroon leaning toward the whites and

aloofness from the blacks, and left him in the camp of
the latter. They, too, had suffered; they, too, had been
wronged; they, too, were entitled to compensation, if
only by way of revenge. He did not know this Don José
Morales except by sight, and by reputation as the
proudest of the old Spanish Creoles, with very poor
credit commercially, and with a daughter whose
beauty was the talk of the town. But he was a white
man, and for this night all white men were Paul
Marchand's enemies; what should happen to them was
no concern of his. They were all his enemies. If he
could make them change places with himself, or with
the two degraded Negroes in the adjoining cell, he
would do it with a holy joy. Perhaps, he thought, after
a while, he might make a few exceptions, but only a
few. He fell asleep again.

He awoke a while later, when everything was still,
except for the stertorous snore of one of his neighbors
and the shrill chirp of a cricket in the wall. Sleep having had a calming effect on his passion, the seriousness
of his own predicament, should Hector Beaurepas
prove vindictive, was even more apparent; and it occurred to Marchand that in this event his knowledge of
the contemplated plot might be utilized to his advantage. To reveal a Negro plot was a public service almost
great enough to counterbalance any misdemeanor.
That he could escape a fine Marchand did not expect;
imprisonment was not unlikely; but he would consider
himself fortunate if he escaped any more ignominious

punishment, and he would do much to accomplish this. But even this course would not be entirely satisfying. The two prisoners, like himself, were martyrs to caste; whatever their characters or their crimes, it was not for these that they were incarcerated, but for the unpardonable and unescapable crime of color. To denounce them would be to condemn to certain death two men who might never have either opportunity or courage to execute their plans.

The rest of Marchand's night was spent in a fitful doze, through which the dawn seemed long in coming.

CHAPTER VII

———⟶●⟵———

Monsieur Renard

I N THE MORNING Marchand sent for his lawyer. While, under the old regime in Louisiana, as under the system in the more northern states, the law provided that a man charged with a crime or misdemeanor should have a right to a speedy trial, the accused was in fact brought to bar when it suited the convenience of the judge, the prosecuting attorney, or others who might be interested in the outcome. The wishes of the prisoner were the last to be consulted. Moreover, the French system regarded solitude, with its opportunities for reflection and meditation, as an excellent thing for a prisoner. The Americans had introduced trial by jury and other innovations, but they had not changed the Creole habit of mind. Being a man of color, with an influential white man interested against him, Marchand realized, therefore, that he might be kept in prison for weeks without trial, and that it behooved him to secure, as soon as possible, the intervention of an equally influential white man in his own behalf.

The lawyer for whom Marchand very wisely sent was the same Monsieur Jules Renard who had provided for his youth. Monsieur Renard's trust had long since terminated—at least Marchand had never called on him for funds since his marriage. But by habit he had always gone to Monsieur Renard for legal advice and service in his business affairs and in the management of his wife's property. A good lawyer, Monsieur Renard would no doubt have sufficient interest in the welfare of a profitable client to make it reasonably certain that he would do everything possible to extricate Marchand from his unpleasant predicament. That it was a matter for influence rather than legal procedure Marchand knew quite well. It might be possible to use money, if necessary and if the bribe were large enough. Henri Beaurepas was a notorious spendthrift, in whom, in case he were obdurate, a sum of money large enough might promote magnanimity.

A piece of silver in the palm of the turnkey brought Monsieur Renard to the prison early in the morning— so early, indeed that Marchand himself wondered that a lawyer of Monsieur Renard's standing should trouble himself to attend any client at such an hour. But the motives which influence human conduct are not always visible on the surface of things, as Marchand was soon to learn concerning others than his lawyer.

Monsieur Renard was admitted to the prisoner's cell.

He stepped forward toward Marchand with both hands extended, explaining with unction, as he advanced, "My dear fellow, this is an outrage! For what can you possibly have been shut up here? It is some mistake. I shall see the magistrate at once."

Marchand wondered at the warmth of his lawyer's greeting. In their former intercourse Monsieur Renard had been always courteous. Your true Creole gentleman was ever the pink of courtesy. He graded his politeness, of course, according to the degree of its object, with a due regard to social distinctions. A wealthy colored client was not a person to be treated otherwise than with consideration. Nevertheless, the courtesy shown to a quadroon, no matter how deserving, was not quite that exhibited toward one of the ruling class who possessed equal claims for consideration. For instance, in their former intercourse, Monsieur Renard had addressed his client as "Marchand" or sometimes as "Monsieur Marchand," the latter itself a distinct concession. Upon this occasion he had accosted him familiarly, but Marchand was quite man of the world enough to know that this betokened no falling off of respect; indeed it was this very fact, combined with a certain air of sympathy which he had never before observed in his lawyer, but of which he was immediately conscious, that made him wonder.

He briefly related the incidents of the evening, including, of course, his visit to the quadroon ball and the reasons for it. Monsieur Renard was elderly and discreet, and would respect the seal of professional confidence. Moreover, the freemasonry of feeling which the lawyer had manifested bred in Marchand a corresponding expansiveness.

"It was a mistake, my dear Paul, a grave mistake," declared Monsieur Renard, with either a real or a well-simulated indignation. "It shall be repaired immediately, and with due satisfaction to your honor. I'll see the magistrate at once."

Monsieur Renard went away, leaving Marchand all the more puzzled. The honor of a quadroon might indeed be a very vital thing, to the quadroon, but it was not usual for a white man, however amiable, to concern himself about something which theoretically could not exist. Under the old regime, when every white man was a walking arsenal, men of color were not allowed to bear arms, and Marchand himself, had he carried upon his person when arrested a sword or pistol or dagger, would have been liable to a severe fine, because of that fact alone. An honor which, in an age of dueling, could not be defended with sword or pistol, was not a thing to be seriously considered. Hence Marchand's anger took secondary place to the perplexity into which his lawyer's conduct had thrown him. Not only was he addressed in terms of friendly warmth by a leading citizen, but credited with and promised satisfaction for an honor which, in his experience, white men had arrogated to themselves as their exclusive privilege.

What Monsieur Renard said to the magistrate is not of record, though the tenor of it may be inferred from subsequent events. At all events it proved sufficient to obtain the prisoner's release, and Marchand, somewhat ruffled in spirit as well as clothing, though his feelings had been slightly soothed by the promptness of his release and the championship of his lawyer, returned to the bosom of his family.

His wife greeted him with an affection well-nigh hysterical. She was a beautiful woman, dark-eyed, petite, on whom the slight strain of African blood left its mark more in a certain softness and pensiveness of expression than in any pronounced Negroid feature. After Marchand had embraced and kissed his wife, he snatched up their youngest child, a baby girl of two, who threw her tiny arms around his neck and cooed with infantile delight, while little Celestine clung to his knees and clamorously demanded her share of attention.

"We did not sleep at all last night," said Julie. "We were in deep distress, not knowing what had happened to you, and fearing the worst, until Monsieur Renard sent word to us an hour ago that you were safe and would soon be here. About ten o'clock old Terence, Monsieur Pierre Beaurepas's butler, came to the house and said his master wished to see you immediately, upon a matter of grave importance. But you were not at home nor could I tell him where you were."

"I can't imagine what business he could have with

me," said Paul. "And no matter. If it was for anything concerning my interest, it can wait. If it concerned his own, he may thank his precious nephew. At what hour did Lizette reach home?"

"Immediately after you were separated," returned Julie. "When you had been taken away, Monsieur Hector Beaurepas came up with the Duc de Nemours, and the signal having been given, would have had her unmask. Frightened by what you had said, she implored him to desist. On the contrary, he insisted. Monsieur Philippe Beaurepas joined them, and having inquired concerning the affair, demanded that she be permitted to depart without unmasking. The duke was appealed to as arbitrator. As became a gallant gentleman, he decided in favor of Lizette, and Monsieur Philippe gave her his arm to the street and sent his own servant home with her, without having seen her face or learned her name."

"It is all the same," said Marchand. "Her name will be all over New Orleans before night."

"But not at all," said Julie. "She dismissed the servant a block from here and came the rest of the way alone. She was not molested, and no one knows of her escapade except Madame Claudine and ourselves. Claudine will say nothing; she has done wrong and she knows it, and would fear to lose a valuable client."

"I hope she'll be silent," said Marchand. "As for Mademoiselle Lizette, we will keep her under lock and key until we sail for France, which will be within a few

weeks. The air of New Orleans stifles me. I am a man—
a free man and not a slave—and I must breathe the air
of a free country. I hate these *sacré* whites!"

"They are not all unkind," returned Julie. "My father
was white, and he left me his property. And Monsieur
Philippe Beaurepas—" "They are merely the exceptions
which prove the rule," returned Paul. "They despise us,
and I hate them all, each according to his own degree
of scorn. Your father was kind in a way, yes; he gave
you his name and his fortune. As for mine, I have not
been permitted even to know who he was. I hate them
all, and I feel that I shall have my revenge for the slights
they have put upon me; I do not know when or how,
but that sometime, somehow, I shall have it."

The excited manner in which Marchand had spoken, so impressed the little Bébé that with eyes big
with apprehension she hid herself within the folds of
her mother's skirt and peeped out affrightedly at this
strange fierce papa, so different from the kinder one
who dandled her on his knees and fed her with
bonbons.

CHAPTER VIII

———⟫●⟪———

The Will

NEW ORLEANS society had resumed its wonted placidity, after the departure of the Duc de Nemours, which took place about a week after the quadroon ball given in his honor, when it was thrown into a state of even greater commotion by the will of old Pierre Beaurepas, the filing of which for probate was duly chronicled in the *Le Moniteur de la Louisiane*. For this fine old Creole gentleman, having successfully stood off the common enemy from the outposts during a long siege of the gout, was at length compelled to capitulate when the disease attacked the citadel, his heart. His death, while a matter of much concern to a small group, had been expected and its effect upon the public therefore discounted. Nor was death so uncommon a thing in New Orleans—a city of malaria, yellow fever, and duels—as of itself to attract any particular remark. The disposition of the Beaurepas estate was, however, so

entirely unlooked for as not only to bring consterna-
tion to a few but stupefaction to the whole community.

By this remarkable document neither Hector, nor
Adolphe, nor Raoul, nor Henri, nor Philippe Beaurepas
was made the heir or the beneficiary in any degree
whatsoever. With the exception that freedom and
small legacies were bequeathed to his household servants, the great bulk of the estate—land, houses,
slaves, ships, stocks, bonds, money, pictures, books
and personal effects—was devised to a man who had
not hitherto been known as at all connected with the
deceased; a man who had been reared as a quadroon,
who had married into the despised caste and had,
moreover, made himself obnoxious to many good people by intemperate speech, and a tendency to intrude
where men of his reputed class were not allowed. By a
codicil, executed shortly before the testator's decease,
substantial bequests were made to the Catholic Church
for the use of its schools, and to the city corporation to
build a hospital.

Even this astounding disposition of the property,
however, was not sufficient to account for all the interest excited by the Beaurepas will. It was no uncommon
thing for a white Creole father to leave a colored child
a substantial estate. Had not Tony Lacroix, the well-
known *rentier* inherited some fifty houses from his father, Colonel Aristide Lacroix? Had not a large part of
the quadroon holdings of New Orleans real estate had

this origin? Was not even the wealth of this pestilent quadroon, Marchand, a bequest to his wife from her white father? No, the lash on the whip of the Beaurepas will which stirred the pulses of New Orleans lay in this—that by the terms of his will Pierre Beaurepas recognized this person, hitherto known on the legal records of New Orleans as "Paul Marchand, f. m. c."— "free man of color"—as his legitimate son, declared that he was white of the pure blood, and requested that he assume his name and place as his father's heir and the head of the Beaurepas family!

There was, of course, an underlying romance. The air of New Orleans was full of romance. The old world superimposed upon the new; the careless mingling of races, the flux and reflux of governments—these and a dozen other things had made the city a center of adventure which pulsed with romance. The will of Pierre Beaurepas did not recount the story, and since it did not at once become public property, the Creole imagination was given full play for the concoction of whatever series of imaginary events might account for so strange an outcome. For, while it was not unknown that a quadroon or octoroon should pass for white, and while it had happened in rare instances that a white child, for whom there was no way to account except with shame and disgrace, had been permitted to grow up as colored, yet there had never been any case so fully authenticated or involving a family of so high a standing.

Those to whom this astounding will came with greatest shock were, of course, the five nephews of Pierre Beaurepas. Picture to yourself five young men, each of whom had built for himself, out of great expectations, a lofty pedestal, upon which he should shine; a tower of Babel, as it were, which should lift him above the floods of poverty or misfortune; and then imagine this lofty structure demolished by a single thunderbolt and its builder left floundering in the ruins, dazed by the shock of the disaster. Or, imagine a man sailing across a placid stream toward a pleasant goal, and that a sudden squall should overturn his craft and leave him struggling in the rough waves. Only some such figure as this could possibly typify the state of mind into which the Beaurepas cousins were precipitated by this remarkable will of their uncle Pierre.

What unutterable disappointment was theirs: into what depths of temperamental despair they were plunged; what maledictions they called down upon the soul of their deceased relative; what sources of consolation they sought to take off the first edge of their disappointment, it would not be kind here to recount. The power of wealth is nowhere more manifest than when wielded by a dead hand. The will of their uncle Pierre, which, had it been in favor of any one of them would have created envy, jealousy and hatred in the others, operated by its totally unanticipated character to unite them for the time being by a common bond of sympathy.

The will had been in the possession of Monsieur Renard, old Monsieur Beaurepas's lawyer, who had announced that he would make its contents known to the
relatives after the funeral. The cousins, with no suspicion of its contents, and masking their jealousy of one
another for the time being, had jointly attended the
obsequies, which were very imposing, the funeral taking place from the cathedral on the *vieux carré*. Clad in
deep mourning they had followed the mortal part of
their dead relative to its last resting place in the old St.
Louis Cemetery, and seen it deposited in the family
tomb. Each had manifested considerable self-restraint;
for each, feeling himself certain to be the heir, would
have been inclined to resent as presumption any apparent putting forward of themselves on the part of the
others, but for a certain pity at the disappointment
which his misguided relatives must shortly endure. Let
them get what little comfort they might from their
fleeting self-deception. The awakening would be more
than cruel enough to offset it.

Upon the return from the cemetery, where the remains of Pierre Beaurepas had been literally "laid on
the shelf," the five cousins, Monsieur Renard, and in
the background the servants of the household, all gathered in the grand salon of the family mansion, and
there waited, surrounded by the portraits of four generations of Beaurepas, to hear what the dead voice of
the family's latest representative should declare as to

the disposition of the estate which these four generations had accumulated.

Monsieur Renard read the fateful document. During
the stupor which fell upon the listeners as the terms of
the will were disclosed, and ere the storm which followed could break loose, the servants were dismissed,
rejoicing at the freedom conferred upon them, and
Monsieur Renard continued.

"Monsieur Paul Beaurepas, *ci-devant* Marchand," he
said, "the heir of the deceased, feeling some delicacy
about intruding so soon upon the grief of the family with
which his connection has been so recently recognized,
has requested me to act as his representative upon this
occasion, and in his name, therefore, I take possession of
this house and the effects of my late client."

When he had spoken, Terence, the butler, his face
aglow with happiness—for by his master's will he had
been made free in person and independent in means—
stepped forward and handed his late master's keys to
the lawyer.

Then the storm burst.

"It is infamous," said Hector Beaurepas, "that our
uncle should leave the estate to a quadroon."

"Pardon, monsieur," exclaimed Monsieur Renard.
"Monsieur Paul Beaurepas, hitherto Marchand, is recognized by the will of my client, as white *pur sang*—of
the pure blood. That he has been reared a quadroon
was a misfortune, for which my late client had an ex-

cellent excuse, but it does not impair the purity of the blood of Monsieur Paul Beaurepas."

"We will not endure it," declared Raoul Beaurepas. "Our uncle shall not disinherit us for this bastard of his, be he white or yellow."

"Again I would remind you, monsieur, that the will of your late uncle, whose remains we have but just now consigned to their last resting place, distinctly describes my present client, Paul Beaurepas, as his legitimate son. And even though there were a technical point involved, bearing upon the question of his legitimacy, this act of recognition of itself establishes, by the civil law, which is the law of Louisiana, the legitimacy of Monsieur Paul Beaurepas. Were he a quadroon, he could take under this will; were he a natural son, this will would yet convey to him the property; but as the recognized legitimate or legitimated son of Monsieur Beaurepas, he would inherit, will or no will; for the proofs of his birth are in my possession, and I am authorized, both by the deceased and by Monsieur Paul Beaurepas, whom I represent, to make them known to all who could have any possible interest."

"We demand them," said Hector Beaurepas. "We wish to know by what preposterous fairy tale we are to be deprived of our inheritance."

Monsieur Renard had a Frenchman's love for dramatic effect. He cleared his throat, and assuming a pose similar to that in which he addressed the court during his most glowing pleas, delivered himself as follows, while his hearers listened, at first with an angry incredulity which, as he proceeded, changed to the settled gloom of unwelcome conviction.

"When I say," said Monsieur Renard, "that the romantic story which I am about to relate involved the good name of a lady, I do not mean thereby to imply any reflection whatever upon the spotless purity and delicate sense of honor which characterized this lady together with all the other ladies of Louisiana. Nothing could be farther from my thoughts, nor would it be safe for me, in a company of Southern gentlemen, to cast any such aspersion upon the sex which we honor and admire. But, as the greatest of English poets has said, 'Be thou as chaste as ice, as pure as snow, thou shalt not escape calumny;' and no degree of foresight or discretion can always guard against accident or the unforeseen.

"For example, let us imagine a case. A lady, fresh from the convent, in the flower of youth, is married, without consulting her own wishes, to a man whom she has scarcely seen. Although her heart has been given to another, she stifles her feelings and in all wifely honor for years performs her duty to the man whose name she bears. But he is unworthy to possess such a treasure. He repays her devotion with coldness; to coldness succeeds neglect, and to neglect desertion. He goes away to fight the pirates in the Spanish Main, some say to join them. He is reported killed, and the report is verified, seemingly beyond the possibility of a

doubt. The desolate heart of the widow turns naturally
for solace toward the one whom she had loved, and
who, remaining faithful to his heart's first choice, had
remained unwed. He pours out upon her all the love
which had been repressed during the years of her cov-
erture. She is not only desolate but in need. He begs
that she give him the right to protect and support her.

"But she is a woman of fine feeling; she respects the
conventionalities. She does not wish to offend public
opinion or render herself liable to adverse criticism by
forming a second matrimonial alliance before the expi-
ration of the period of mourning which convention
and decorum seem to require; for she was of an old
family and proud, as our Creole ladies are justly proud.
But the gentleman was pressing; her needs were also
urgent—how urgent none but herself could know. She
yielded at last to her lover's importunities, and they
were married privately, in a distant parish. Returning
to New Orleans they resumed, to all appearances, the
usual current of their lives.

"But man proposes, and God disposes. Events took
such a course that three months later madame began to
think that it might be well to disclose her marriage, in
order to avoid harsher criticism than that which would
follow a too hasty marriage—which would be, after all,
but a slight thing as compared with one supposed to
have been too long deferred. She had agreed with her
husband that the marriage should be announced the
following day. But ere it was made known the impossi-

ble happened—her former husband made his appearance in New Orleans. The report of his death, though made in good faith, had proved to be not in accordance with the facts.

"I need not ask you to picture the situation or to put yourselves in the lady's place. It was a case for heroic remedies. Innocent of wrongdoing, her good name must not be impaired. But how could it be protected? Her marriage was no marriage. Even her husband's return would not protect her; the period of his absence from the city was too well known. Upon this score, however, fortune favored her, at her husband's expense. Two days after his unexpected return, he was stabbed in a brawl in a Canal Street gambling house, and she was left a widow in very fact and deed. The marriage ceremony was thereupon repeated in still another parish.

"But this merely relieved her of one embarrassment; there still remained the other, which the new marriage could not cure. There was but one remedy—concealment. To save the mother's good name, it was necessary temporarily to sacrifice the child. The lady retired to a distant plantation. The child was born and placed at nurse in the hands of a discreet quadroon woman, herself ignorant of its origin, and supposing it to be the child of a white father by some woman of her own class. The child's wants were amply provided for, through the medium of a discreet man of affairs, himself unaware of the real facts.

"It was the intention of the parents, after their re-marriage, to adopt the child. Before the step had been taken, however, the revolution in San Domingo sent to New Orleans, among the refugees from that unhappy island, five nephews of the father of the as yet unac-knowledged child—three sons of his brother René and two of his brother Louis. To have adopted a fatherless child, to the disinheritance of his own flesh and blood, would have caused curious and unfriendly comment. Madame Beaurepas—and I need not carry the parable further, since the word is out—with her high sense of honor, her strict view of propriety, her delicate sensi-tiveness to public opinion, had grown morbid upon the subject of this unacknowledged son. Her nervous system broke down, and she became a chronic invalid. At any mention of her son the intensity of her emotions was such as to threaten her life. To spare her, the day of acknowledgement was allowed to remain indefi-nitely in the future. Upon her death my late lamented client, out of respect for her memory, chose still to keep the matter secret until his own death, which brings with it the recognition of the rights of my pre-sent respected client, Monsieur Paul Beaurepas, who, I can say without fear of contradiction, though brought up to suppose himself a quadroon, was always amply provided for, was carefully educated, and is prepared at every point to take up the responsibilities which have so suddenly been thrust upon him. If there have arisen seeming obstacles to this, growing out of the misconception of his race, they are not such as the law, in its wise and humane provision, cannot and does not correct.

"The story has been told to my client, Monsieur Paul Beaurepas. Indeed I asked him to be present here today, and from the next room he has heard all I have said to you."

At this, Paul Beaurepas, late Marchand, f. m. c., stepped into the room and bowed courteously to the other gentlemen, only one of whom returned his salutation, while the others glared at him with undisguised animosity. Monsieur Renard continued:

"With the chivalrous courtesy which distinguishes the men of Louisiana, Monsieur Paul Beaurepas has uttered not one word of blame for his father or his mother. A Creole gentleman, he is willing, in the retrospect, to have sacrificed even his life, had it been demanded, to save the honor of a lady, and especially of a lady who bore him so close a relation. A dutiful son, he bows to his father's will. The late Monsieur Beaurepas honored me with a measure of his confidence. It was through my agency that he provided for the support and education of his son, although I did not at the time know certainly what their relationship was. At his request I drew up this very will, leaving blank the name and description of the chief legatee, which you will observe are inserted in his own handwriting. Not until he took to his bed, ten days before he died, did he take me into his full confidence, and then only because he

wished me to convey to his son certain information
which he had not seen fit to embody in his will. Monsieur Pierre Beaurepas assured me, in our last interview, that he had always kept track of his son and
would have intervened to protect him in case of any
threatened danger or misfortune. Indeed, he sent for
him upon his deathbed, but unfortunately, because of
events that evening, with the story of which you are all
familiar, was not able to reach him. I should have been
pleased to serve professionally whomsoever my late lamented client had chosen to be his successor. I have
accepted with satisfaction and with pleasure the position of legal advisor to his heir, Monsieur Paul Beaurepas, and shall do what I can as friend and advocate to
make up to him what he has lost by virtue of the temporary obscuration of his name and social standing."

During the progress of this oration there were murmurs of incredulity, expressive shrugs and shaking of
the head among the nephews. It was a pretty story, but
it would not, to use a significant American expression,
hold water. It was manifestly a scheme of their malicious old uncle Pierre to divert the family estate, which
he in his turn had in large part inherited, from its lawful heirs, his nephews, to this quadroon by-blow, and
to cover up this act of robbery by this fairy tale con-
cocted at the expense of a lady who was dead and gone
and therefore unable to defend her honor.

CHAPTER IX

———⟫●⟪———

The Five Cousins

Paul beaurepas, late Marchand, f.m.c., had listened to the lawyer's statements with a countenance the immobility of which cloaked a variety of emotions. When Renard declared him fitted in all respects to wear the mantle of the late Pierre Beaurepas, and hand on the traditional glory of his race, whence came the shadow that flitted momentarily across the pale olive of his cheek? When the lawyer announced that his client had no word of blame for his dead parents, was it a flash of resentment that for a moment lit up his dark eyes with a lambent flame? Or was it the glow of a chivalrous acceptance of his sponsor's statement? And when in his closing remarks Renard referred so delicately to the removal of seeming obstacles, was it regret which saddened the face of Paul Beaurepas, or tenderness which moistened his eye with a film so light that a single movement of the lids dispelled it?

Upon Marchand's appearance the cousins had instinctively drawn together at one end of the salon. Monsieur Renard had turned to his client and stood awaiting the compliment which he had expected and which came in grave tones from the lips of the heir.

"A noble deliverance, Monsieur Renard, replete with wisdom and legal learning and a delicate sense of honor and its obligations. With such an advocate, there can be no situation too difficult to meet, no obstacle too great to overcome."

Monsieur Renard bowed low to the quadroon of yesterday—today the heir of Beaurepas. If there were any sarcasm in his client's voice, it was not perceptible to Monsieur Renard, the astute lawyer, the eloquent advocate, who could read the mind of a witness like an open book; for here there was nothing at issue, nothing in doubt. As his client had said, there could be, in a matter which should naturally give rise to pleasant and indeed joyful emotions, no embarrassment which Monsieur Renard's advice would not clear up. He had unfolded an interesting mystery in a dramatic way, had elucidated a delicate situation in a masterly manner, which had given his forensic powers full play; and he was but receiving his due meed of appreciation, which he expected as certainly and valued as much, in its own way, as the substantial fee which later on he would collect from his highly respected client.

For, from the first interview in the Calabozo, Monsieur Renard had seen the importance of binding to himself, while yet he was alone in the field, this new

fledged great proprietor. His business as Marchand had
been worthwhile; as Beaurepas it was vastly more important, and having conducted it for the father, it was
no more than natural that he should wish to retain it
for the son. Nor was he moved only by self-interest, but
by a sincere desire to serve. He had always liked Paul,
and liked him none the less now that he had turned out
rich and powerful. With genuine pleasure and good
will, therefore, he looked forward to guiding, with tact
and delicacy, his client's untried feet in the new paths
where they must tread. Diplomacy would be needed to
adjust the new Beaurepas to his changed environment.
For Monsieur Renard, with his knowledge of human
nature, its weaknesses, its limitations, knew instinctively that although Paul Beaurepas, hitherto
Marchand, had lived and moved and had his being in
the same city which held within its borders the forty
thousand people who made up all the grades of this
curiously stratified community; though he had walked
the same streets, breathed the same air, spoken the
same tongue, read the same books, worn the same
clothes, yet that in the kingdom of the mind, of which
these other things were but the mere integument, he
had lived as truly in a different world from that to
which he had now received legal title of admission, as
though a gulf as wide as the ocean and as deep had
rolled between them.

The one particular wherein Monsieur Renard foresaw a possible difficulty of adjustment, he had referred

to, somewhat obscurely so far as the mere words went, but quite intelligibly to Paul Beaurepas, when he had spoken of the legal removal of certain seeming obstacles. Monsieur Renard had already told Marchand, prior to the funeral, that it had been the wish and the intention of old Paul Beaurepas, although not made a condition of the inheritance, that his heir should marry the daughter of his old friend José Morales and through her perpetuate the family name and lineage. There was, fortunately for the plan, no legal obstacle. In some of the more northern states, or in France, to which the Creole eye turned instinctively when it looked abroad, Paul's marriage to Julie Lenoir would have been valid, but the law of Louisiana made it illegal and void, and Marchand could repudiate it without legal or social reprobation and proceed to carry out his father's wishes should he so desire.

Nevertheless, Monsieur Renard had felt rather than foreseen that he might have difficulty with his client upon this point. Acting under instructions, he had followed, through a Paris correspondent, the student career of Paul Marchand in that city, and knew that he was a man of sentiment; that he had been an ardent Republican and had accepted and proclaimed the radical doctrine of the Rights of Man as applying to all men, with no reservations. Indeed Monsieur Renard had had occasion once, shortly after his ward's return to New Orleans, to caution him because of some intemperate remark, reported to Renard, reflecting upon the moral-ity and the economic soundness of slavery. His client, too, he had learned by inquiry, was a devoted husband and a fond father.

As a lawyer, Monsieur Renard had found the man of sentiment a dangerous client, likely, under the stress of sudden emotion of quixotic impulse, to upset the most carefully devised plan of attack or defense—to throw, to use a modern industrial figure, a monkey wrench into the machinery. It was far easier to handle a man who was swayed solely by self-interest, who would obey the rein and neither take the bit between his teeth nor kick over the traces. And Monsieur Renard was not entirely certain his client was a man of this latter class.

The group at the other end of the salon conversed in subdued but animated tones. They were, with one exception, unanimous in their condemnation of the will and their hostility to the heir.

"Our uncle was a monster!" exclaimed Raoul bitterly. "He led us to believe that we would inherit, and then cut us off without a picayune."

"Nay, cousin," said Philippe Beaurepas, "he has told each of us, many a time, that we need not hope to inherit."

"But he told us each separately—not together; and there was no one else to inherit, so far as we knew. It was wicked, it was devilish to treat us so."

"A man," said Philippe, "can do as he likes with his own. It is a well known maxim of the law."

"But there is another equally trite," retorted Raoul.

"A man should so use his own as not to injure that of others. He had led us to cherish false hopes, and then he dashed them—after having waited, like a coward, until he was beyond the reach of our reproaches."

"And he has added insult to injury," interjected Hector, "by leaving his money to a quadroon."

"He is a Beaurepas of the pure blood," protested Philippe. "The proofs show it. There he stands beneath our grandfather's portrait. He might have sat for it."

They turned their eyes toward Paul, who stood listening gravely to the smooth flow of Monsieur Renard's words and apparently paying no attention to the group of cousins, no word or movement of whom, however, had escaped him.

"He has been bred a quadroon, and blood without breeding is not enough to make a gentleman. He would disgrace the name by some Negro trait. He has been trained to subordination, to submission. How could he resent an insult? No such man can maintain the honor of the Beaurepas."

If Honor ever blushes, as poets have asserted, she must have done it then. Only the day before, Henri Beaurepas had sold the mother of his unborn child, to whom he had promised her freedom, to pay a gambling debt!

"He has suffered more than we," said Philippe, stoutly. "What each of you may lose, beyond the hope of wealth, I know not. I shall lose the dearest hope of my life, and I value this money not one whit except as it might have enabled me to realize this hope. Our new cousin gains the estate, but what does he not also acquire with it? The knowledge that he has been robbed, for all these years, of the sweetest things of life—a father's name, a mother's love—of gentle breeding, of honor and renown, of the companionship of his equals—robbed of them all, too, in that happy third of life, when they are most valuable, when the fortunate youth must shine by reflected light, ere he has been able to accomplish his own career."

"A mess of sentimental nonsense," sneered Hector. "You talk like an actor in a melodrama. The fellow was bred a quadroon and expected nothing better."

"He will go back," said Philippe, "for he is a man of imagination, he will go back and live over all those years in retrospect and suffer every pang which his ignorance had heretofore spared him. He has my sympathy; but for one thing, I would rather be myself than he. I shall give him my hand, and welcome him into our family."

There were murmurs of dissent, but Philippe heeded them not. He even shook off a detaining touch and walking the length of the hall, held out his hand to Paul Beaurepas, who clasped it warmly.

"Cousin," said Philippe, "your accession to your own has dashed my fondest hopes. But it was no fault of yours. I welcome you as the head of our house, and bespeak from you the friendship and interest which a cadet has a right to expect from the head of his family."

Paul Beaurepas had watched the hostile group gloomily, and somewhat wistfully. His face had lightened at Philippe's approach, without losing all its gravity.

"I thank you, cousin," he replied. "I shall not forget your loyalty and you shall not regret it. You were my well-wisher I liked to think—I would not have dared to call you friend—when I had no claim upon your good will."

He shot a hostile glance toward the group at the other end of the hall, who lingered, casting furtive looks toward Philippe and muttering sarcastic comments.

"My brother and my cousins," said Philippe, "are terribly disappointed. I hope you will not judge them too harshly."

"They will feel more resigned tomorrow," said Monsieur Renard, softly, rubbing his hands. "They will consult eminent counsel; they will see that my client's rights are unassailable, and they will think of other things which will make them reflect ere they go farther."

The group of disgruntled cousins turned to go. "Pardon me," said Philippe, "if I go with them, and try to reason with them."

When they were gone Paul Beaurepas drew from his inside pocket a little red morocco-covered memorandum book, and turning to a list of names, struck one of them off with his lead pencil.

Monsieur Renard prattled on. His client seemed preoccupied, but some of Monsieur Renard's words, the lawyer felt sure, if only one here and there, would fall on fertile soil and bring forth fruit.

"You will no doubt wish to go through your father's papers, and may find something about which you will wish to consult me. Meanwhile I shall file the will for probate."

Which he did, and, as we have seen, to the surprise and wonder of all New Orleans.

CHAPTER X

———➤●◄———

Julie and Her Chickens

JULIE AND her children were gathered in the living room of the family home on Bourbon Street, which had come to her from her father. Jacques Lenoir had been a man of culture, as evidenced by the books on the walls, most of which had been his, and of discriminating taste, as shown by the choice of the pictures and art pieces which decorated the room. There was an open piano, with sheet music on the rack, a harp, and on the table some current French novels and magazines. The interior was not so magnificent as that of the Beaurepas home on Royal Street, but the intimate touches of life and the presence of the children, made it much more comfortable, though Julie did not know it, having never been in the other house.

She was seated in a low chair, a prey to sadness. She had not seen her husband for a week and was beginning to feel anxious about him and about the future. Even the children observed her distress.

"What is the matter, maman?" babbled Bébé, coming to her mother's knee and gazing concernedly into her face.

"Yes, *petite maman*," said Celestine, "your eyes are all red. You have been crying. Your handkerchief is wet with tears. Is it about papa? Has anything happened to him? We haven't seen him for a week. What can be the matter with him?"

The little mother nerved herself for an important communication. Her ivory-tinted face, whose soft contours were generally alive with cheerfulness, took on an unusual sobriety. The fate of her children, to say nothing of her own, was trembling in the balance. Lifting the long lashes which shaded her dark eyes, she turned upon her two children—two smaller images of herself, two doll-like creatures, clad with French daintiness in little white muslin frocks, with sashes of broad ribbon, their little heads covered with luxuriant curls which fell in natural ringlets to their waists—a look surcharged with emotion.

"My poor children!" she exclaimed, with a tragic air.

"Yes, mama," they cried, with vague premonitions, echoing her tone and mirroring her expression.

"We have met with a great misfortune—a terrible calamity! Your papa is—"

"Our papa is dead!" they cried, bursting into loud wails.

"No, my children, it is not so bad as that, for your papa, but for us it may be worse."

"What is it, mama?" demanded Celestine.

"Prepare yourselves, my angels, for terrible news. Your papa is—"

"Our papa is—"

"Your papa is—white!"

Loud was the weeping, as Julie gathered her chickens under her wings. Their papa had hated white people. Celestine had heard him declaim fiercely against their prejudice, their arrogance, their brutality and, more particularly, their slights of himself. Only a few days ago they had even heard their father swear a great French oath, that if all the white people of New Orleans had but one neck, and he could hold it in his hands, he would strike it through at a single blow, or wring it like a pullet's—b-r-r-r-r, zip! At least, he had added a little later, after supper and a glass of wine, he would be tempted to do so. That their father should be one of these wicked white men was truly a dreadful thing.

Julie was very unhappy. She loved her husband and knew that he had loved her. But he had possessed her, and now he might leave her. She was a quadroon, and he might take to wife any one of the many beautiful unmarried white women of New Orleans—it was inconceivable that any one of them should refuse the hand of one so handsome, so distinguished and so rich. But his good fortune was her undoing. For her sake and her children's she wished he were still a quadroon. They would have gone away and been happy.

Now they must stay in Louisiana, and she saw no way of reconciling the future with their happiness.

She consulted her confessor, Père Ambrose, but he, poor man, could give her no comfort. He was in the grip of the same forces which controlled them all, and the ghostly vice-regency[1] of Heaven could not avail against the Louisiana code. He could only repeat the stale formula of his creed and adjure her to love God and keep his commandments, and intimate, without quite saying it, that if temptation proved too strong for her and she should sin, the church would not refuse her absolution nor make her penance unduly severe.

CHAPTER XI

———⟫●⟪———

The Black Drop

Paul Beaurepas, after taking possession, as we have seen, of the family mansion, went through his father's papers. The deeds, contracts, notes and securities, of which there were many, were on deposit in the vault of the Bank of New Orleans, but in his father's desk there were numerous diaries, commonplace books and memoranda dating back for many years, throwing light upon the history and traditions of the important family of which he was called to be the head.

If he came upon any obscure point upon which he desired information, Terence, who had acted in part as his late master's secretary, and whom Paul had retained in his employment, was often able to clear it up. He had grown up with Pierre Beaurepas and knew almost as much about the family as his master—with the exception of some few things, several of which are important to this story.

Among the many letters which the late Monsieur

Beaurepas had preserved, there was a small packet, tied with a faded blue ribbon, in which Paul found a letter from Haiti, dated during the Revolution, and addressed to Pierre Beaurepas.

Paul read the letter with interest, and from it learned several things. The letter[1] was written by Laure Beaurepas, the wife of Pierre's brother René, and had been penned during the horrors of the Revolution, as its uncertain handwriting and overwrought tone gave ample evidence. The writer's husband, it stated, had been killed by the insurgents, with tortures unnamable. The writer herself had been wounded, but had escaped, with her children, by the aid of her faithful servant Zabet. Dying, she confided to Zabet her three young children, together with two of her husband's brother, Louis Beaurepas, with injunctions to carry them, if possible, to their uncle in New Orleans.

"To you, my dear brother, as head of their house," she wrote, "I confide my dear children. May God deal with you as you with them, and may a mother's blessing and the love of God follow every good thing which you may do for them. I dread most leaving the little one—the others will be stronger and more able to care for themselves; but I trust in Christ and the Virgin and in you."

The letter gave Paul food for thought. He had already learned from his investigations that the parents of his cousins had been ruined in the Haitian Revolution. From this letter he gathered the manner in which his cousins had come to New Orleans. One clause only was obscure; where the writer had spoken of the little one, she had used the feminine form, "*la petite*." His five cousins were all males. Was this a grammatical error, due to the writer's stress of emotion? Or, if not, who was the girl, and what had become of her, and whence had come the fifth male cousin? It was a subject too delicate to question Terence upon directly, so he merely asked the butler if the late Monsieur Beaurepas had ever had a niece, to which question Terence returned a negative answer.

The next day he sent a servant for old Zabet. She came smiling and curtseying, expecting a reward. Had not her prophecy been fulfilled? Was not the former quadroon now white, and rich and powerful, and in the way to obtain all the rest that she had promised him? Surely he would be liberal, nay, more than liberal, even generous.

"Good day, Zabet."

"Good day, Master Paul. My dream came true!"

"It was no dream, Zabet. Your prophecy came true in part, and you shall be rewarded—that is, when you shall have answered me three questions."

"Three hundred, master, if old Zabet could know so many things."

He motioned her to a seat. She sat down upon the edge of it, and watched him shrewdly through narrowed eyes. His aspect was serious, not to say severe, and she felt vague forebodings.

"When you left Haiti with the children of my uncles, there were five. How many did you bring to New Orleans?"

"Five, master; three of Miché René and two of your uncle Louis. Have you not five cousins?"

"What became of the little one, the girl?"

Zabet turned pale; her eyes narrowed to two slits.

"The girl, Master Paul?" she stammered. "There was no girl. I brought only boys. Everyone knows it; they have grown up in the house. They are known to all New Orleans."

"Yes, Zabet, but when you left Haiti, there was a girl!"

"No, master, five boys! I swear it! Five boys, Raoul, Hector, Adolphe, Henri and Philippe, five nephews of your father, Pierre Beaurepas! I swear it before God and the Virgin! May I be struck dead in my tracks if it be not so!"

Paul Beaurepas was not satisfied. Zabet protested too much; she was as much too vehement as too palpably afraid.

He rose, went to the door and locked it. Zabet followed his movements with a fearful curiosity. He took from a closet a rawhide whip, such as overseers used to chastise slaves, and from a drawer a pistol, which he loaded and primed deliberately, and from a hook where it was suspended, his sword, and laid them side by side on the table.

Zabet followed his movements with the fascination

of terror. What did he mean to do? Old Pierre Beaurepas had been a hard man, but with a vein of cynical
humor and with lapses of humanity. This new Beaurepas's face was set like a stone mask. Zabet's flesh began
to creep with apprehension, which was only partially
allayed when Beaurepas drew from another drawer a
rouleau of gold pieces, which he placed beside the
weapons.

"Zabet," he said, "you are my slave."

"But, master," she stammered, "I am free—my mistress gave me my freedom."

"You are my slave, Zabet. You were never legally
freed. You are mine, by inheritance from my father."

"He never claimed me—I have been free for thirty
years."

"Then if you are not mine, you belong to my cousins."

"God forbid!" muttered Zabet, crossing herself.

"You see upon the table an inkstand, in which is a
pen, with one stroke of which I can transfer you to a
slave dealer. You are old, but still capable of much hard
work."

"Mother of God, save me!" whispered Zabet.

"There is here a whip. If with it I should beat you to
death, no one would have a word to say!"

"You would not do it, master," she moaned. "There
were five boys—I swear it!"

"With one stroke of this pen, I could write an order
to Valdez, at the calaboose, to loosen your tongue."

Zabet trembled. Never in her life had she been

whipped, but she knew what such an order meant, and knew, furthermore, that none could gainsay it. So Zabet trembled and the blood in her veins stood still.

Beaurepas went on, coldly and incisively: "A touch of this pistol, a thrust of this sword, and you would go to meet your God, Zabet, with all your sins upon your soul."

Zabet had no wish to die. She had not confessed for a month, and there had always been reservations, held for her last confession. Nor did she wish to give up life; too old to sin, she could still enjoy the savor and cherish the memory of past offenses.

"Master," she muttered shakily, her eyes evading his, "there were five boys."

Paul Beaurepas strode over to the trembling hag and seized her by the arm.

"Down on your knees, huzzy!" he thundered. "Down on your knees and tell me the truth, or take your choice—the slave gang, the whip, the pistol, or the sword."

With one hand he forced her to her knees, and with the other reached toward the table.

"There were four boys, and a girl, master, when I left the island."

"Ah!"

Paul Beaurepas released his hold on Zabet's arm and left her groveling on the floor.

"Go on!" he said, "go on!"

"The little girl died—there were too many, the ship

was small and crowded, the sea was high, the sun was hot, the water was stagnant, there was no milk—the little girl died."

"Who was the fifth boy?"

"Your uncle René's child, master, and my daughter's! His child as much as any! I brought the child with me, and when the little girl died, I brought the boy instead to Pierre Beaurepas—who was also *his* uncle!"

A look flashed over Beaurepas's face, a look which boded ill for someone, though not for Zabet, for the tone in which he now addressed her was kind. Having won his point he could afford to be magnanimous.

"Get up, old woman," he said, lifting her to her feet. "You have told the truth. One question more, and one more truthful answer, and the roll of gold is yours. Which of my cousins was the fifth child?"

Zabet's face fell. "Master," she pleaded, "you'll not be hard on him? You know what it is not to be white?"

"Oh, no, Zabet. I shall do to him no more than he deserves. His name?"

She whispered a name in his ear. The sinister look, which had disfigured his countenance and might very well have marked the joy of anticipated revenge, gave place, after Zabet had spoken, to an expression very like disappointment.

CHAPTER XII

——➤●◄——

The Honor of the Family

DESPITE HIS outward calm, Paul Beaurepas, during the weeks which had passed since the discovery of his birth, had gone through a fiery furnace of emotion. No one but a man of spirit finding himself in that condition could quite have known what it was to belong to an inferior caste in a city like New Orleans. Even the Negroes retained a measure of natural dignity and self-respect, which slavery had not been able to eradicate entirely and which yearned dumbly for recognition, and the proud blood of French gentlemen, even when mingled with that of slaves, sometimes clamored for its birthright.

He had lost so much! He had enjoyed much, it is true, in comparison with others less fortunate; but we too often measure our happiness by what we lack and not by what we have. Paul Marchand, free man of color, had possessed a certain degree of wealth and education. He had therefore resented all the more fiercely

the deprivation of civil rights and social opportunities.
His pride had in a measure sustained him; but one
man's pride was a weak barrier against a whole world's
scorn, and to Paul Marchand and all who dwelt within
its borders, the Crescent City was the world, and the
white people within it the people thereof. The others
were permitted to live, like the slaves, because they
were useful to the whites, or, as the free people of
color, by sufferance. Slave or free, they had no rights
which white men might not override. That there was
left to those who were free some measure of comfort
and pleasure; that not all white men were tyrannical
and unjust; that the quadroons were envied by the
blacks far more than they were despised by the whites,
consoled some of them, but had never satisfied Paul
Marchand. Whether it were blood or temperament, he
had cared very little what the Negroes might think of
him—he had pitied them with a profound pity, but
had never counted himself as one of them. Thus, between two castes, he had grown into a proud isolation,
which had developed into a bitterness that the revelation of his birth could not all at once assuage, but
rather, as Philippe suggested at the reading of the will,
even tended to accentuate.

As had been predicted by Monsieur Renard, the
cousins took counsel among themselves and with lawyers, and decided that discretion was the better part of
valor. In the consultation it came out that each of them
was heavily indebted to the estate. The purpose of old

Pierre in bringing this about was so obvious that no one of them imagined for a moment that Paul did not have the notes of hand they had given their uncle. Having been advised that a contest of the will would prove futile, that there was no possible ground for claiming that undue influence had procured its making, and that both church and state were interested in maintaining its validity, their interests obviously required that they placate the heir, in order that the tradition of the house in reference to the younger members should not be broken. It was decided to give a family dinner at the home of Henri, at which their new cousin should be the guest of honor. It was, in effect, the ancient service of fealty. They would acclaim their cousin as the head of the house, break with him the bread of hospitality, and drink to his happiness in the wine of fellowship. No formal invitation was issued, but Philippe undertook the task of inviting Paul to honor the occasion with his presence. Paul signified his assent with the grave dignity which had marked his manner since his sudden accession to wealth and social position.

It was a men's party. Henri chanced to be in funds, and the table was elegantly appointed. The dinner, sent in from a hotel, was prepared by a *cordon bleu*, and served by well-trained waiters. The conversation was general, and upon topics of current interest, seeming to avoid by mutual consent the matter of inheritance and the circumstances attending it. The formal part of the entertainment was reserved until after the coffee had been served. At this point Henri Beaurepas, who had been chosen as spokesman, having filled his glass, rose to his feet and cleared his throat. Instantly silence reigned and every eye was turned upon him.

"Gentlemen and cousins," he began in conventional phrase, "we are gathered together here on this auspicious occasion to unite in an act which we owe to the honor of our house and to the memory of our distinguished relative and benefactor. By a strange fate, for which no one of us is responsible, our cousin Paul Beaurepas, having been for many years deprived of his birthright as the son and heir presumptive of our uncle Pierre, has come into his own. If any of us had been led, through ignorance of the real facts, to anticipate a different disposition of our uncle's estate, it too was equally with no fault of ours. The Beaurepas family has long been one of the glories of Louisiana. It took its root with the birth of the colony, and we all hope that it may survive and maintain its prestige so as long as this fair city shall stand. Its fate, for the next generation, rests in the hand of our relative, Monsieur Paul Beaurepas, our honored guest upon this occasion. That he may prove more than equal to this responsibility is our earnest wish, our fond hope, and our confident expectation.

"As cadets of this distinguished family, it will be our duty as well as our pleasure to hold up the hands of our fortunate relative in all things that may tend to maintain the honor and dignity of our name. As younger members of the family we desire to feel ourselves free to seek at the hands of the head of our house that sympathy and support which his commanding position will so well enable him to extend. We have therefore gathered here tonight to cement with friendship the ties of blood which already unite us to him. Gentlemen and cousins, I propose the health of our cousin, Paul Beaurepas!"

The toast was drunk with much show of enthusiasm, and when the glasses rested again upon the table all eyes were turned toward Paul. He rose from his seat and spoke with the gravity which had characterized him for the past week.

"Gentlemen and cousins," he said, "I thank you for this expression of loyalty toward one whom fate has so suddenly and unexpectedly thrust into your lives and the life of your family—*our* family. Such a tender of fealty demands an adequate response. Ordinarily there could be but one reply to such an offer. But the very unusual circumstances of my upbringing, for which I find no fault with anyone, have created on my part a situation equally unusual, and impel me to make a somewhat different course from what might be expected. No one could know so well as you the Beaurepas crest, a mailed arm erect, the hand holding a sword, with the motto "*Coup pour Coup*"—"Blow for Blow," nor could anyone so well as you appreciate the principle which has always governed the Beaurepas in affairs of honor. That principle is, as our motto implies and as you well know, that an insult can only be wiped out with blood. Other men, with milk in their veins, might accept an apology for a blow—words for deeds—but no Beaurepas has ever yet accepted an apology without having first crossed swords with his insulter. I take it that I can do no less than maintain the honor of my house—*our* house—nor can I imagine for one moment a scion of that stock acting upon any other rule. Before, therefore, responding to the toast which you have drunk to me, I deem it my duty to search the history of my past and see if there is between myself and any gentleman here present any matter which involves the honor of my family, or of myself as its representative. If there be, then I know that no one of you would ask or expect of me such a compact of friendship until this cause of offense has first been removed."

The Beaurepas cousins were looking at one another with wonder in their eyes. What bee had this regenerated quadroon in his bonnet? What card had this parvenu Beaurepas up his sleeve? What did it all mean?

Vague memories stirred within them. They were not long kept in suspense. Paul Beaurepas drew from his breast pocket a small morocco-covered memorandum book, which he opened and held before him in the light of the wax candles which shimmered in the chandelier above the table.

"I have here," he said, "a little memorandum, made

by me at various times during the past year, by reference to which I find that on the first of October last, at
the instance of Monsieur Henri Beaurepas, a lease
which I had taken of a box in the second tier of the
opera house was canceled; that on the second of Janu-
ary, on the complaint of Monsieur Adolphe Beaurepas,
I was refused service in a restaurant on Canal Street;
that on April the tenth I was slapped in the face by
Monsieur Raoul Beaurepas on the *vieux carré* in front of
the cathedral; that on the fifteenth, in a dispute with
Monsieur Hector Beaurepas, in the cotton exchange,
he called me to my face a Negro, and a pig, and said
that he would slit my ears, but that it would defile his
sword; again at the instance of Monsieur Henri Beaurepas, I was ignominiously expelled from a ball at the
Salle Condé, on which occasion, in defending myself
from unwarranted assault, I happened to strike Monsieur Henri, and, also at his instance, I presume, I was
incarcerated in the Calabozo, where I spent several unhappy hours. Some of these were small matters, perhaps, or might at the time seemed to have been, but
can I, as a Beaurepas, enter into a compact of friendship with gentlemen, however closely related, who
having thus offended me have not satisfied, in the traditional way, the honor of the Beaurepas?"

There was never a more astonished company. This
cousin of theirs, while yet to all intents and purposes a
quadroon, had treasured every slight, had marked it

down with day and date; and to what end? He could
have had at that time no inkling of his birth or prospects. For what reason, except for a hypothetical revenge which he could have had no probable means of
realizing, could he have pursued such a course? To
their superstitious minds it almost appeared as though
some supernatural influence had taken this cousin of
theirs under its protections and led him to do instinctively this curious and dangerous thing. It was a proof,
too, if any were needed, of his purity of race. No quadroon could have taken such a course; it was foreign to
the quadroon nature.

Henri Beaurepas was the first to find speech.

"Cousin," said he, conciliatingly, "we perceive with
pride that our uncle's mantle has fallen upon worthy
shoulders. You have justly stated the unwritten law of
our family. But to even so well established a rule there
may be exceptions. By the law, as I have been advised,
the intention is an essential element of the offense. If
perchance in passing through a crowded street I acci-
dentally brush against a gentleman and cause him to
lose his footing and fall, judged by my lack of intent I
have committed no offense for which an apology
would not be ample satisfaction. If, on the contrary, I
have of set purpose and with hostile intent but laid the
weight of my little finger upon a man's person, I have
committed upon him an assault which the law would
punish by fine and imprisonment, and which by the
code of honor could only be wiped out by an abject

apology or by blood, and by the Beaurepas code, by blood alone."

"By blood alone," echoed Paul, softly.

"But, cousin," continued Henri, "applying this rule, there was in your case no intent to offend. To us Paul Beaurepas did not exist; and we could not insult one who had not come into being. The acts of which you complain were directed against a certain *soi-disant* quadroon, who, in his turn, no longer exists. A white man could not insult a man of color, and therefore there was no insult."

"Pardon me, cousin, Paul Beaurepas—I who speak to you—was not born yesterday, but twenty-five years ago. It was this cheek," he said, laying his hand against it, "it was this same cheek that tingled with the blow. It was these ears which burned with the offensive epithet, and which would have listened to the music of the opera. It was these feet which carried me into the ball-room; it was these bones, gentlemen, which lay upon the cold stones of the calaboose—they are sore yet from the contact; it was these lungs that drank in the vile air of the prison. And it is this cheek, these ears, it is all these that clamor for satisfaction. Gentlemen, I echo your wish that there shall be none but pleasant relations between us. But my conscience will not permit me to accept your friendship until I shall have proved my title to the honor of a Beaurepas."

Philippe was next to speak.

"Our cousin Paul," he said, "is right. He could not do

otherwise. He has not called my name. But if I have at any time offended him, though unwittingly, I am ready to accord him the satisfaction of a gentleman."

"Our cousin," added Adolphe suavely, "does not, I am sure, thirst for our blood. To cross swords with us will be enough to satisfy his honor—the honor of the family."

"It is his right," said Hector, "and we acknowledge it. It is brave of our cousin thus to stand upon his right. For we, because of our upbringing, are skilful with the sword, while he, because of his, can have no familiarity with it. Nevertheless, he would defend his honor at any risk. I think I speak for all of us when I say that this meeting or these meetings will be but a mere formality, for no one of us would take advantage of our cousin's want of knowledge of the gentleman's weapon."

"Certainly," they all assented. "It will be but a mere formality."

If Paul Beaurepas, late Marchand, felt any inclination to smile as he listened, it was indicated by nothing more than an almost imperceptible parting of the lips.

"Gentlemen and cousins," he said, "I thank you. That you could give no other answer I well knew, and that I could take no other course was equally apparent. As the challenged, it is your privilege to name the time and place of meeting."

"Since there are four of us and but one of you," said Raoul, "we waive the privilege. Fix your time and place and we will be in attendance."

"The Oaks, with swords, at six o'clock, day after to-morrow morning," said Paul promptly. "Tomorrow is the Sabbath and we will wait until Monday."

"Our new cousin," said Hector to Henri, when Paul had gone away, "seems to take the family honor *au grand sérieux.*"

"It is a new toy, and he likes to play with it," returned Henri. "Then, too, it is the zeal of the proselyte—he wishes to do something spectacular and un-African to make people forget the Negro that he was."

"He is either very stupid, or very subtle," replied Hector. "We shall have to watch our step."

"It is a matter," said Henri, "for deep thought. Our cousin, too, had best be careful."

CHAPTER XIII

———❖———

A Tip from Perigord

ADOLPHE BEAUREPAS, sauntering idly along Royal Street on Sunday afternoon, on his way to the *Café des Exilés*, where he had an appointment with a San Domingan gentleman, to arrange the details of a cock fight, met Guillaume Perigord, the fencing master.

"*Bonjour, Monsieur Beaurepas*," exclaimed Perigord with the military salute which he affected.

"*Bonjour, Perigord*," returned Adolphe. "How do you carry yourself?"

"Very well, thank you. And you, monsieur?"

"Passably. What could you expect, after an earthquake—a revolution. The cursed will of my uncle—"

"Ah, yes," returned the other with seeming sympathy. "It was astonishing, almost incredible. But truth is stranger than fiction. And the duel—it is curious, what I have heard, if it be correct?"

"What have you heard, Perigord?"

"*Pardieu*, that Monsieur Paul Beaurepas is to meet each of his five cousins tomorrow morning, consecutively, in satisfaction of certain insults which he received as Paul Marchand, free man of color."

"It is true, Perigord, but—"

"I wonder he is not afraid! The Beaurepas are good swordsmen. Five to one are large odds."

"Certainly, Perigord, but it will be a mere formality. It is a tradition of our house that for an insult one must fight. Our cousin must, for the honor of the family, cross swords with us. It will be a mere formality—our cousin's upbringing has not been such as to give him skill with the gentleman's weapon."

"Ah, that is well. Your cousin has great confidence in your magnanimity. He has so much at stake! If the duel were *à l'outrance,* who knows what might happen? A stroke, a thrust, and the estate would descend a second time, all in a week—but, then that would do you no good; your cousin is married and has children who would inherit."

"Not so, Perigord! As a man of color, he was married; as a white man, he is not. His wife is his mistress, his children bastards. Were the meeting a real one, or should there be an accident, the estate would go to the legal heirs, his cousins."

Perigord smiled grimly. The Beaurepas cousins were known by reputation to all New Orleans, and there had been few to sympathize with their chagrin.

Adolphe started to resume his walk.

"But, Monsieur Beaurepas," suggested the fencing master, with a seriousness of tone which masked a sly smile, "it is well, too, for Monsieur Paul's cousins, that this meeting is a mere formality."

"And why so, Perigord?"

"For a very good reason. I will tell you a secret— Monsieur Paul Beaurepas is the best swordsman in New Orleans."

Adolphe Beaurepas's mouth opened wide with surprise, and stood open until, with an effort he found speech.

"But it is impossible! He has been brought up colored, and colored men do not bear arms!"

"You forget that he was educated in Paris. I knew him there; he was a pupil of Jaures, my own master. Even Monsieur Henri Beaurepas cannot touch him. I have seen him put five men *hors de combat* in ten minutes. He was at my *atelier* last night, practicing with me certain difficult passes."

Adolphe endeavored to conceal his surprise, as, repeating the remark that the meeting was a mere formality, he left Perigord and went on down the street. This news of Perigord's was disturbing, to say the least. That Paul Marchand-Beaurepas was a skillful swordsman might well be—in a Paris *salle d'armes* a quadroon might fence with a nobleman. But why should he be practicing passes with a fencing master? Did he suspect treachery, and mean to be on his guard against it? Or did he secretly cherish some deep scheme of revenge, and mean to wipe out the whole family? Adolphe himself was a poor hand with the saber. The possibility of accident had been foreseen, by the challenged cousins, but Adolphe, with the rest, had rather expected that such an accident might take place in the encounter with Henri. It had indeed been arranged that Adolphe should first cross swords with the challenger, then Raoul, then Hector, and then, when the formal character of the meeting had been completely established, an accident might happen which would change the succession. They had not actually planned such a thing, but the possibility of it had been in the minds of them all.

But suppose that Paul Beaurepas were vindictive? He, Adolphe, would be at his mercy; he would be first to meet him. If *he* should be the victim of an accident—the prospect was not so pleasing! If he were not present, he would run no risk. Suppose the worst—or rather, suppose that Paul Beaurepas should kill one of the cousins, or two, and then, wearied by his efforts, should fall by Henri's sword? Adolphe could only profit by such an event. In no way could he suffer by remaining away from the meeting, and in no way could he profit by warning his cousins. If one or more of them were killed, there would be fewer for the head of the house to favor. If the head of the house succumbed, he, Adolphe, would share the estate with the others without running any risk; in the very improbable event of the whole party being wiped out, in a miniature battle of Roncesvalles, he, Adolphe, would be the sole heir to the Beaurepas millions!

But these reflections, however pleasing, were but dreams. He turned back to where the fencing master was standing looking after him quizzically.

"As I have said, Perigord, it will be a mere formality. Please say nothing to the others, if you meet them, about my cousin's skill. There's no need to disturb their equanimity. The meeting will be a mere formality, to satisfy an imaginary point of honor."

CHAPTER XIV

⟫⟨⟩⟨⟫

The Duel

THE MEETING which Paul Beaurepas had demanded of his cousins took place at The Oaks,[1] the fashionable Creole dueling ground, a cleared vacant space several squares north of the cathedral, marked by three large water oaks. While the place and time of the meeting had not been advertised, enough about it had leaked out to draw a small knot of curious spectators, who kept themselves in the background, however, behind the screening shrubbery which surrounded the dueling ground.

The gentlemen met and exchanged formal greetings. There had come of Paul's five cousins only four. Philippe was present, though not among those challenged.

"Our cousin Adolphe," suggested Paul, "will doubtless appear later. Shall we wait or proceed?"

"Let us go on," said Hector. "He will appear."

"I will answer for him, cousin," said Philippe.

At that moment a colored messenger came up and handed Paul a note.

"Pardon me, gentlemen," he said, as he broke the seal and glanced at the writing, which he thereupon stuck in his belt. The gentlemen had removed their coats and waistcoats and were in their shirt-sleeves.

The contestants had agreed to fight without seconds. There being no mortal offense, it had been agreed that the character of the meeting would permit them to dispense with some of the usual formalities. Henri Beaurepas, representing the challenged had selected sabres as the weapon, to which Paul had assented. Nothing had been stipulated as to the length of the swords, and if Henri Beaurepas had provided himself with an unusually long one, Paul Beaurepas gave no sign of having observed it.

"Are you ready?"

Raoul Beaurepas advanced and drew his weapon.

"On guard!"

After a few preliminary passes their sabers clashed. Pass followed pass, thrust was countered with thrust. Raoul was a good though not a brilliant fencer. Paul Beaurepas, handling his weapon in what seemed to the casual observer an awkward manner, kept to the defense for several minutes, but finally, as their swords clashed in midair, Paul's weapon seemed to slip downward and the point made a slight wound in Raoul's left cheek.

It had been agreed that the drawing of blood on either side should end that particular encounter.

Paul Beaurepas was profuse in his apologies.

"My cousin Raoul, and you, gentlemen, will pardon my awkwardness. It is due, of course, to my ignorance and lack of skill, the result of my upbringing. I could have deferred this meeting, of course, until I had taken a few more lessons and could have met you on more nearly equal terms. But you are doubtless as anxious as I to get these little matters out of the way, and to that end will consent to undergo any temporary inconveniences attending the process."

"It is nothing," said Raoul. "Were this a real encounter I should be ready to go on."

"No," returned Paul, "I am satisfied. By a rare coincidence my sword has scratched you in the precise spot where you so impulsively struck me in the *vieux carré*. Who is next?"

Hector Beaurepas stepped forward.

"On guard!"

This Beaurepas, the most quarrelsome of the family, was a better swordsman than Raoul. Moreover, he was beginning to suspect that Paul Beaurepas was more skilled than he would have them believe, and was therefore strictly on guard from the moment their swords clashed. He made stroke after stroke, tierce, carte, thrust and counterthrust, each of which was parried by Paul with seeming awkwardness but with unvarying success. At length Paul assumed the offensive, Hector defended himself cleverly, but finally in a sudden and seemingly awkward lunge which Hector sought unsuccessfully to parry, the edge of Paul's sword slit the right ear of his adversary downward from the top for about half an inch.

"*Pardieu*, cousin!" exclaimed Hector angrily—he was boiling with rage and could hardly contain himself—"but you are most damnably awkward. You might have put out my eye. Deliver me from amateur fencers!"

"I crave your pardon, cousin. It is but a little thing—no more than you said, at the cotton market, that you would have liked to do to me had you not feared to defile your sword. It will leave only a slight scar, and I have not soiled my sword. I am entirely satisfied. I trust you bear no malice?"

Hector grumbled something which might have been an assent and stepped to the rear.

"And now my cousin Henri? I shall have to watch myself with you, cousin, or I shall come off second best. On guard!"

Henri Beaurepas had no longer any illusions about the swordsmanship of his cousin Paul. That he was a good fencer, a better one than either of the men he had met, was perfectly plain. His pretense of awkwardness did not deceive Henri, nor was he any longer in doubt as to his cousin's purpose. This contest was no mere formality. It was being fought by Paul Beaurepas with a definite, though so far obviously not a deadly intention, and Henri was determined to secure, if possible, the advantage. His purpose was less pacific. Aside from any question of the estate, his reputation as a swordsman was at stake. He was quite willing to kill his cousin if he could.

He set out to force the fighting, but the first few passes convinced him that he might as well dismiss his sinister purpose, and that he would do well himself to escape maiming. He tried every form of attack—the press, the lunge, the thrust, the riposte—but all were met and foiled. He feinted, but never caught Paul off his guard. His long sword could never quite reach his adversary. He tried several tricks which he had learned from Perigord, but Paul seemed to sense them at the first movement and met or parried them all.

As the fighting grew fast and furious, the spectators pressed forward from behind the shrubbery, until the contestants were surrounded by a ring of eager faced young men who added by their cries and applause to the excitement of the occasion. Finally, in making a rather low thrust which Henri tried unsuccessfully to parry, the point of Paul's weapon found lodgement in the upper part of his adversary's thigh.

Henri dropped his sword and clapped his hand to his wound.

"It is too bad," said Paul ruefully. "I am very sorry. You will need a surgeon."

At this moment a man with an instrument case made his way to the fore.

"I took the liberty," said Paul, "of asking Dr. Duchesne to be in attendance, in case I might require his services for myself, or lest awkwardness, in spite of the best intentions, might have some such untoward result as indeed it has had. But it is partly your own fault, cousin Henri. You are the better fencer and you pressed me too hard. Your sword, too, is much longer—I shudder to think what would have happened had you proved awkward. I trust the wound is not serious, doctor?"

"No," replied the surgeon, "but he will not be able to dance for a month or six weeks."

"'Tis a great pity," returned Paul, "for no one loves so well as he to dance. The Salle Condé balls will miss him. But, gentlemen, I think this terminates our meeting."

"Not so," said Philippe, who had been an eager spectator. "My brother Adolphe has not arrived."

"He has sent a note," replied Paul with an imperceptible smile, as he drew from his belt the paper which the boy had brought him. "He writes that, owing to a touch of inflammatory rheumatism in his sword arm, he regrets most profoundly that he must ask me to defer our meeting until some later date."

"But the honor of the family," said Philippe, "is not satisfied. Since Adolphe is not here, I will meet you in his stead. You have been offended, you are entitled to satisfaction, and I will not permit my brother to defeat you of it."

"But I've no quarrel with you, cousin," returned Paul. "Your honor is not impugned by his absence."

"But that of the family is. You are the head of the family, but not the sole custodian of its honor and traditions. We also bear the name. I shall assume my brother's obligation and cross swords with you in his stead."

"As you will," replied Paul, indifferently.

They placed themselves on guard. After a few passes, by a quick stroke, Paul sent Philippe's weapon flying about ten feet beyond him. Philippe recovered it and would have gone on.

"No, no, cousin," said Paul, "it is enough, and you have saved your point. You have done a gallant and chivalrous thing. I admire your spirit, but have not the heart to fight you. I do not want your blood, nor do I wish you to draw mine. I have upheld the family tradition and wiped out my insults in blood—a very little of it was enough—and I have nothing but the kindest and most kinsmanly feeling for you all."

These were fair words, if not, in view of what had just happened, entirely convincing. A carriage had been brought for Henri, and he was driven away for further attention. The other gentlemen, followed by a crowd of spectators who had gathered during the altercation, made their way back to the city.

THE duel, or rather the wholesale meeting between Paul and his cousins, created only a less sensation than

had the will of old Pierre, and the community was kept
as busy guessing about it as certain of the Beaurepas
were in explaining. Paul was the most talked of man in
New Orleans. That a man, reared as he had been,
should stand up face to face against four gentlemen
born and bred, and place them all *hors de combat*, was
a wonderful thing, and not entirely explained by the
theory that the cousins, out of deference to their cousin
Paul's lack of swordsmanship, had permitted him to
slit the ear of one, gash the cheek of another, and to
well-nigh hamstring a third, reputedly the best fencer
in New Orleans, not to mention disarming the other.

Nor was the explanation that the meeting was a
mere formality at all convincing. That a man should
slice several others up more or less completely, and
seemingly at his own sweet will, as a mere formality,
was even less likely than that four fire-eating Beaurepas
should willingly submit to such treatment, especially
with the odds so much in their favor. Adolphe Beaurepas's absence from the meeting was the subject of caus-
tic comment, his rheumatism was openly scoffed at,
and his reputation suffered still further by some reference by Perigord at his *atelier* to their conversation before the duel.

There was less said to Paul Beaurepas than to anyone
else concerning the matter. His manner did not invite
confidence or familiarity. Those who had scorned him
as a man of color felt some natural delicacy about
forcing themselves upon him as a white man. It was

felt that it would be better to leave these matters to time and circumstance. They would, of course, adjust themselves.

CHAPTER XV

———⟫●⟪———

Don José Pays His Respects

DON JOSÉ MORALES called upon the heir of Beaurepas soon after his succession.

"Monsieur," he said, "I wish to pay my respects to the son of my old friend. I wish it had been my privilege years ago. I have heard your father criticized for leaving you so long in ignorance of your birth. But he was my friend; do not think too harshly of him."

"Never fear, Señor Morales, I have not uttered one word of reproach against him. Did he not, by the stroke of his pen, lift me from the painful condition of quadroon—a Negro—to the exalted position of the best white family in Louisiana, excepting, of course, your own? He might never have told me. I might have always remained a quadroon and worn out my heart with useless repining."

"You are a good son, and will make a good father."

"I am a father already."

"Ah, yes," replied the old Spaniard with a fine smile, "we know—young blood flows swiftly in our climate. But you must have sons to inherit the name and the estate of Beaurepas; it is a duty you owe to your family and to society."

Paul Beaurepas smiled to himself somewhat grimly. So far at least, the debit side of his social account was not of impressive magnitude.

"You will make a good father, if you have the right mother for your children. Come out to Trois Pigeons and see us. Your father came every month. My daughter will be glad to know you. Your father loved her."

"Thank you, Don José, I shall come."

Old Morales still lingered.

"By the way, Paul—I shall call you Paul, I called your father Pierre—there was a matter between your father and me."

"A matter," he returned.

"Yes, a mortgage on my plantation. It has been running many years, and I fear the interest is somewhat in default. May I hope that you will be as lenient as your father?"

"Do not disturb yourself for the present, Señor Morales. I have not yet looked thoroughly into the affairs of the estate. Until I am better informed do not disturb yourself."

This was not strictly true, but he had not cared to anticipate what he foresaw Don José had come to say. He had learned, of course, of the mortgage on Trois Pigeons, and was entirely familiar with the state of the account, but for certain reasons did not wish to commit himself at this time.

Old Morales went away, relieved but not entirely satisfied. He had hoped that Philippe would be the heir of Beaurepas, or if not Philippe, one of the other nephews, with a provision conditioning the inheritance upon marriage with Josephine, or at least, a clause forgiving the debt. But none of these things had happened. Pierre Beaurepas, with his malicious humor, must have chuckled to himself upon his deathbed at the prospect of the complications to which his will and astounding revelations attending it would give rise.

"He was my friend, but if I am broken," mused old Morales, as he rode away, "if I have to give up Trois Pigeons, I shall say he was a damned scoundrel. He led me to think I should never have to pay the debt, and then he dies and leaves it to a stranger, his son—he says—he is the image of him, and he has no sign of Negro blood—but at heart an alien to our race and caste. I am between the devil and the deep sea. This Beaurepas is smooth-spoken; his words are very dutiful, but not once in our interview did he refer to old Pierre as his father. I am not sure of him, unless he shall come to see Josephine. She is beautiful, and few men could resist her. I have promised her to Pierre for his heir. It is a pity about the other woman, but—what of it? She is a quadroon and that ends it. She can be provided for; it is done every day."

He rode home, dismounted, threw his bridle to a slave, and sought his daughter. He found her pale and hollow-eyed, with traces of tears upon her cheeks.

"Josephine," he said, "all is not yet lost, but whether or not we shall leave Trois Pigeons and face ruin depends upon you."

"Oh, father, I can do nothing. Philippe was disinherited."

"It is not a question of Philippe, my child. Philippe, as you say, is disinherited. As he had understood all along, he was to marry you if he were the heir. But Pierre Beaurepas has tricked us all; Philippe is not the heir and therefore you are not for him."

"But I love him, father."

"Silence, Josephine! No well-bred maiden should love where she cannot marry. There is another; the heir himself has promised to come and see you."

"Father!" exclaimed Josephine with indignation, "a quadroon to visit me—to visit us!"

"*Peste*, Josephine! The man is no quadroon, but as handsome a white man as we know."

"But he has a wife."

"A quadroon wife, my dear, whom neither the law nor the church recognizes."

"But they have children!"

"Quadroon children, my daughter, bastards. Their mother's status fixes theirs."

"I could never bear the sight of him," declared Josephine. "He has been brought up as a Negro. He must feel as a Negro, think as a Negro; I could never be sure of him. Besides, father, I love Philippe!"

"I forbid you to love Philippe," said Morales, sternly, "and order you to make yourself agreeable to the man whose word can make us paupers. I promised you to old Pierre's heir, and by God, I shall keep my word!"

Josephine said nothing, but cried her eyes out, and waited for Philippe. But Philippe had not come; indeed, her father had sought him out, after the will was published, and frankly stated the hopelessness of his passion, and had forbidden him the house.

So Josephine cried her eyes out, but Philippe did not come. She sent a letter to him by a slave, and received a reply by the same means. The messenger dared not risk his hide by taking another—he stood in mortal terror of Mendoza's lash. So Josephine cried her eyes out, and stopped between her tears only long enough to eat and sleep; for rarely does youth lose its appetite for either. And she swore that if her father married her to this white-quadroon, or this quadroon-white, she would give him cause to regret his choice—she loved Philippe and would never love any one else!

CHAPTER XVI

At Trois Pigeons

ONE MORNING, glancing at the daily newspaper, Paul gave a mighty start. An item on the first page announced the escape, from the city prison, of two prisoners—a Negro and a mulatto—who had been arrested two weeks before as runaways, on the plantation of Trois Pigeons, and sentenced to be sold as vagrants. They answered to the names of Jean Lebeau or *Grande-Tête*, and Pedro Valdez, or *le Borgne*—the one-eyed. A description of their persons followed, with the statement that a posse had been sent in pursuit of them.

Paul's memory ran swiftly back to the colloquy he had overheard in the Calabozo, between the inmates of the cell adjoining his own, and a swift vision rose before him, of a broken levee and a wide plantation flooded; of a house in flames, and of a young woman at the mercy of two wretches brutalized by slavery, maddened by unjust imprisonment, burning with the fire of revenge. Paul Beaurepas had a substantial interest in

Trois Pigeons plantation; in fact, it belonged to him whenever he chose to claim possession, and any damage to it was an injury to himself. But not for one moment did this view of the matter occur to him. The danger to Josephine dwarfed every other thought.

He recalled the plot he had overheard in the prison. He had not the slightest doubt that the escaped prisoners would make their way toward Trois Pigeons. They were desperate men—like Ishmael, every man's hand was against them, and theirs against every man. Sure to die, sooner or later, by violence, they would live only to gratify strong passions—lust and drink and gaming and revenge. By sacking Trois Pigeons they might sate them all. Even now, thought Paul, they might be killing the master and the overseer, firing the house, or cutting the levee.

He hastily summoned old Terence and ordered his best horse saddled and brought around. Buckling on a sword and thrusting a pistol in his belt, he mounted and rode away toward Trois Pigeons.

It had been raining for several days. The road was muddy and the riding hard, and Paul's good horse, pressed to its utmost, was tired ere he reached the outskirts of the plantation. As he neared the river and looked across the cotton fields he saw men running toward the river, with spades and shovels in their hands. The first step had been taken. The miscreants had cut the levee, and quick work would be necessary to save the bottoms from inundation. The next step in the plot would be to watch the house until none were left in it but the women and children.

Paul had scarcely turned where the road led to the house, when he saw a dark figure running through the shrubbery. He caught only a fleeting glimpse of the runner, but enough to show that he was going toward the house, and seeking to keep himself concealed. Hardly had he disappeared when Mendoza, Don José's overseer, came galloping up.

"Monsieur," he said, "I do not know who you are, but I crave your assistance. The levee has been cut, and unless the water can be stopped, the district will be flooded."

"Who is at the crevasse?" demanded Paul.

"Don José himself, with the Negroes."

"Can they hold it?"

"For a while, perhaps."

"Then come with me to the house," cried Paul, "for a greater danger threatens—fire, and worse."

As they rode forward, he rapidly explained the situation. Mendoza scowled fiercely, and with his right hand fingered the handle of his knife which rested in his belt.

"Ah," he remarked grimly, "they want revenge. Well, they shall have it, on the wrong side of their faces."

Rapidly they rode forward. The road by which they advanced was much longer than a direct line would have been, so much longer that when they came at length in sight of the plantation house they heard a medley of screams and wild shrieks and saw a flock of women scurrying out of the patio. A moment later a huge mulatto dashed from the house with a woman's limp form thrown across his shoulder, and simultaneously a thin column of smoke shot out from an open window.

The mulatto no sooner caught sight of the two white men than with a cry of rage he sprang into the shrubbery with his burden. Paul dared not fire at him for fear of striking Josephine; and in the shrubbery a horse would be a useless encumbrance. He dismounted, followed by Mendoza. Simultaneously a cry of fire rang out.

"Damnation!" cried Mendoza. "I must save the house, while you look after the señorita.[1] One white man is equal to ten Negroes."

Nevertheless, as Mendoza entered the house, the Negro desperado, standing behind the door, brained him with an ax. The overseer had lived by violence. He had made himself the instrument of the greed and avarice of others; he had done the dirty work of slavery, and had paid the price at the hands of one of the victims of the system. We never borrow but we must pay. Sooner or later the scales are balanced.

Paul followed the fleeting mulatto and his burden, and soon caught up with them. In spite of his huge strength, the man had wearied of the load. He stopped, and held the girl up before him, while with the other hand he drew a knife.

"Stop!" he said, "I'll parley."

Marchand stopped.

"Stand where you are until I have gone a hundred yards, and I'll drop the girl. Advance, and I'll cut her throat."

Here for the first time, in an emergency, Paul's quadroon training pushed itself to the front. The ordinary white man at such a juncture would have seen nothing but a white woman, in the grasp of a black brute. Paul Beaurepas—for the moment Paul Marchand—saw, beyond the evil countenance of the man who had faced him, the long night of crime which had produced this fruit—the midnight foray in the forest, the slave coffle, the middle passage, the years of toil beneath the lash, the steady process of inbrutement which the careless endowment of white blood had intensified by just so much vigor and energy as the blood of the master had brought with it. He must save the woman, but he pitied, even while he condemned, the ravisher. Only a few weeks before, he himself had said, purely as a figure of speech, that if all the white race had but one neck, he could cheerfully wring it. To what extent could he blame this victim of a race's sins, who had suffered so much more, if he should seek to do to one of them what Paul Marchand had recently thought of as to all?

And this pity was very nearly his undoing. For while he paused, the second desperado, still bearing the bloody ax with which he had slain Mendoza, crept up behind him. Some instinct, or else some hidden change in the mulatto's expression, warned him in time to see the uplifted weapon, and by a quick sidewise spring, learned in fencing, to avoid the blow. Ere the Negro could recover from his frustrated effort, Marchand had drawn his sword and run him through.

The mulatto, seeing his scheme foiled, hesitated, lifted his knife over Josephine's fair throat, and then with a lingering remnant of pity, threw her limp body to the ground and disappeared in the underbrush— sure, wherever he went, to be so long as he lived the bane of the society which had produced him.

Marchand ran to the unconscious girl, and lifting her in his arms started toward the house, before reaching which he met Don José and one of his retainers.

"My daughter," cried Don José in anguished tones, "my daughter!"

"She has fainted, that is all. The scoundrel has done her no harm. He has escaped, but his companion is dead, out there in the bushes."

"And Mendoza?"

"Lies dead within the door, and the house is on fire. We must put it out."

Paul laid Josephine upon the ground beneath a shady tree. One of the frightened Negro women came up, and took charge of her mistress, while Paul joined Morales in putting out the fire. Fortunately, the roof was fitted up with a tank, with a linen hose attached, which, strange to say, was in working order, and the fire, which had not gained much headway, was extinguished with no great difficulty.

When Josephine had recovered consciousness, Señor Morales presented Paul, who had first taken time to remove some of the smoke from his face and hands.

"Josephine," said her father, with a well-calculated expression of really sincere emotion, "behold your preserver—*our* preserver! To him you owe your honor and your life, and I Trois Pigeons!" Which was true in more senses than one. "In him behold the worthy son of our dear old friend and benefactor. He came to call upon us for friendship's sake, and so opportunely that there is nothing we would not do for him. Is it not so, Josephine?"

Josephine glanced shyly at her preserver. He was wonderfully like Philippe, but graver, and somewhat older. He did not look in the least like a quadroon.

"Monsieur is very good," she said politely, "and I am very grateful."

"Take her, my boy," said old Morales, embracing Paul with enthusiasm. "It was your father's wish and my promise; and more, she is yours by right of conquest. You have won her by the strength of your right arm."

At this moment Josephine, for whom events were moving too rapidly, created a diversion by a sharp exclamation of pain, and at the same moment a servant ran up to say that the levee was safe, so Marchand was not compelled to reply. He remained at Trois Pigeons for several hours, however, until Josephine had been put to bed for her nerves, and Mendoza's body had been decently laid out for interment, after which he rode slowly and thoughtfully back to the city. Josephine was very beautiful. A month before he would scarcely have dared to look at her. Today he had held her in his arms. It was not a case where distance lent enchantment, for this close proximity but enhanced her charm. It would have been next to impossible for any man, with red blood in his veins, and certainly impossible for any Creole gentleman under thirty, to hold Josephine Morales in his arms for two minutes without being powerfully moved.

They buried Mendoza on a little hillock that rose in the field. The Negroes never went near the place except in groups, and it was said among them, with bated breath, that the overseer's ghost, with gory head cleft in twain, and carrying his heavy rawhide slave whip, still haunted the cane brake, looking for stray Negroes upon whom to wreak revenge for his own undoing.

———➤●◄———

CHAPTER XVII

Paul's Dilemma

THE IMPASSIVITY which had characterized Paul Beaurepas's demeanor since his new birth had masked a
seething caldron of emotions, and had been achieved by
very great effort. No more radical change in one's life
would have been possible. In one moment, by the
stroke of a decrepit old man's pen, he was raised from a
man of color to a white man. What that might mean in
the South today is at least conceivable to any thoughtful,
observant person who reads the newspapers. The reader
must have already gathered something of what it meant
in New Orleans in 1820, but to make it entirely clear a
little further explanation may not be amiss, even at the
expense of some repetition, because any merit which
this story may have as a social study must depend upon
a reasonably accurate knowledge of the conditions
which surrounded those who figure in it.

Under the old regime the *gens de couleur* or colored
people of Louisiana were a separate class, inferior to

the whites, but superior in the eyes of the whites, and vastly more so in their own eyes, to the Negroes, who were not only black but mostly slaves as well, while the people of color were in large part free. The term "Negro" was never applied to them directly except by way of insult. The term "colored" meant, in common parlance, as now in Latin America, and elsewhere than in the United States, of mixed blood.

Among themselves distinctions of color were jealously guarded, the quadroon or three-quarters white outranking the mulatto, the octoroon or seven-eighths white taking precedence of the quadroon. The term "quadroon," however, was generically employed to distinguish the class or caste.

Men of color, like the pseudo Paul Marchand, were often men of affairs and of means, merchants, landlords and planters. Some of them, like Marchand, were educated in France, where they sent their children to be taught. Some of them remained in Europe, and some returned to Louisiana. Like the white Creoles, they had a strong feeling of local attachment. They were denied civil and social equality, including the right of intermarriage, and they were not admitted to the professions, but beyond these limits the amenities were as a general thing fairly well observed when the men of the races met for business or otherwise.

The women of color were in a more precarious position. Many of them, moved by a perverted social ambition for themselves or for their children, preferred to be white men's mistresses rather than marry men darker than themselves or even of their own degree of color. When their children became white enough it was not hard to cross the line and pass for white. Many of the quadroon women, however, secured the same result, for themselves and for their children, by attaining honorable marriage and moving to France, where there were no social distinctions based on color.

The lot of the free quadroons, therefore, might seem to have been enviable, compared with that of the black slaves. But the very privileges they enjoyed, and the refinement of feeling that grew out of them, only made them more keenly alive to the things they were denied. Under the older French regime this had not been so noticeable; the Latin affinity for darker races, the Latin gaiety, had softened the lines of caste, had permitted much kindliness of feeling among masters and slaves, and had recognized the ties of kinship among the mixed people. But the advent of the more northern American had changed all this. Bringing with him an exaggerated scorn of dark blood, his ideas had quickly given color to the public thought.

In this transition period, the quadroon felt the pressure most keenly. To the slave these changes meant little. At the lowest stage of human fortune, he could sink no deeper; he had reached the bedrock of degradation, so far as he or anyone else could see. Having never had any privileges, he had none to lose. To the quadroon, every old right denied, every former privilege withheld, was but pushing him back deeper into the mire. For instance, the free colored battalion had rendered gallant service in the War of 1812. Its disbandment, in deference to the growing sentiment that to bear arms was the prerogative of white men only, was a bitter blow to the quadroon pride. In earlier days certain boxes in the opera house were open to the quadroons. Their relegation to the gallery, with the Negroes, had been a keener blow than the denial of the suffrage or the right to serve on jury had ever seemed. A man might vote but once a year; it was the little daily slights that stung.

Among the more thoughtful of them, when they came together, the conversation turned always, sooner of later, on the melancholy theme of their wrongs. The ever present grievance tinctured every thought. The great currents of life, the movement of nations, the advancement of science, the development of art, already dwarfed by distance from great cities, were as nothing to the questions of whether a quadroon could eat at a restaurant, attend the theater, or take precedence, in colored society, of a mulatto or man of a lesser degree of white blood.

Some of the quadroons found comfort in a semitropical lethargy; others in the debauchery to which in part they owed their origin. Some managed to hold up their own heads by looking down on those beneath them.

Into this unnatural and painful position Paul Marchand's lot had been cast. In youth it had not been so bad. There was music and love and the hope that springs eternal in the heart of youth. During the few years he had spent in Paris, he had well-nigh forgotten that he was anything less than a man.

For a time he had dreamed, over there in France, that he might return to New Orleans and preach the doctrine of human equality, not offensively, but persuasively, appealing to men's reason and their sense of justice. He soon learned that this was impracticable, if not impossible, and that the condition of his own existence was that he should accept the established order and be content with the place assigned to men like him.

The lesson had not been easily learned. His self-respect had clamored for its life. When confronted by the inevitable, he had, for a time, taken refuge in the weaker position, that by force of the preponderance of his white blood, he ought to be a white man; that it was an outrage that the undistinguishable drop of black blood which lurked somewhere beneath his skin, should degrade him to the position of a man of color.

He might have passed for white. The city had grown so rapidly during his absence that upon his return from Europe he could, with a little friendly reticence on the part of his acquaintance, have easily lost his identity and established a new one. But this chance he had forfeited by marrying a quadroon woman and accepting the ban of the caste. His wife had brought him wealth.

Nevertheless, such is the perversity of the human heart, that he was not entirely satisfied with the bargain. He loved his wife and would have kept her in all honor and respect, and her patrimony had placed him in the ranks of the financially well-to-do, and yet he would have exercised the rights and enjoyed the privileges of a white man. The effort to transmute this mental attitude into concrete action had landed Paul Marchand in the Calabozo, from which his father's death had opportunely released him.

But now all this was changed. As by magic, the door hopelessly sealed had opened and he had been drawn in. The pauper in the world's best things had become the prince who could command them all—great wealth, high social position, unlimited opportunity. Moreover, he was free to marry again, for, by the law of Louisiana, the marriage of a white person to a person of color was null and void. By the stern rule which placed race above every other consideration, a man might father his own slaves, and sell the unfortunate fruit of his loins in the market. He might increase the quadroon caste to any limit, but without the sanction of church or state, nor did either church or state do aught to prevent it. By a legal fiction, which grew into a habit of thought that was to last for generations to come, a man was black for all social purposes, so long as he acknowledged or was known to carry in his veins a drop of black blood. By his accession to the white race, Paul Beaurepas, formerly Marchand, f. m. c., became, *ipso facto*, an unmarried man, and by virtue of his wealth and position as the head of the great family, an eligible aspirant for the hand of any unmarried white woman in Louisiana.

And Julie, and her children? If he so chose, they must accept the inevitable. Julie's birth had not been wrapped in mystery nor had her life been colored by romance, except that of Paul's love. Her parentage was well known, and she bore upon her shapely features, in the warmth of her tint and the wave of her hair, the faint though quite distinguishable imprint of her mother's race. No matter how sweet or desirable she might be as a woman, no fairy tale could make her white, nor could she be a white man's lawful wife in Louisiana.

And Julie's children? Curiously enough, Marchand found himself thinking of them as *her* children. A week before, they had been *his* children. He had not only loved them, but had been proud of them—now he could only be ashamed of them. They belonged in the category of surreptitious things, not to be spoken of, except perhaps among boon companions, in the mellow hours when wine had unsealed the lips, and men were merely men and good fellows.

To say that Paul was not strongly tempted would be untrue. The beauty of Josephine Morales was the topic of New Orleans. A dozen of the young bloods of the city would cheerfully have fought for her, given the opportunity; but Philippe Beaurepas was the only one who had more than a speaking or a dancing acquaintance with her, and her fate had been fixed almost from her birth. She was the price of Trois Pigeons, and no man not able to lift its mortgage might dare raise his eyes to her. This was no delicately veiled family understanding, such as might exist among a colder, more hypocritical people. With her father's pride of blood and her own dower of beauty, Josephine was frankly in the market, for sale to the highest bidder. Philippe had been the favorite, by reason of his expectations. With Philippe out of the way, the field was open to another. Provided he were rich enough and of good family, neither youth nor beauty mattered on his part, nor tears nor regrets on Josephine's. As race was above mere vulgar justice or humanity, so pride of blood and possessions were above any so inconsiderable a thing as love.

To Paul Beaurepas, then, this beauty had been offered—thrown at his head, so to speak. For old Morales was not troubled by fine distinctions of sentiment. The man was white, he was of good blood; his financial position was unassailable, and he held a mortgage on Trois Pigeons for more than the plantation was worth. It was inconceivable that one brought up as Paul had been, to whom white women had been taboo, should fail to appreciate or even to exaggerate the worth of Josephine's hitherto forbidden charms.

But to Paul, Julie was the fly in the ointment. To leave her, to give back the wealth he had received with her, now a mere pittance beside his princely inheritance, would, he feared, break her heart; and he loved her too well to wish to hurt her. That she would be content to live under his protection, and see another woman claim him as husband, he did not believe; nor would he have cared to lead a double life, however easy a lax code of morals might make it, nor could he have respected a wife who could condone such a course. It was one or the other; he must choose between the two. If he married Josephine, he must definitely renounce Julie. If he gave up the thought of marriage with any other woman, Julie might perhaps be satisfied to count their marriage as good in spite of the law, and to bear, for love of him, the odium which attached to an unlegalized connection.

While he wrestled with his problem, during the two weeks which elapsed since the reading of the will, he had not slept at home, spending his days at his office and his nights at the house he had inherited, where old Terence, retained upon wages, waited upon him and gave him an insight into his late master's affairs. He had written several times to Julie, brief notes, to say that he was busy, and that he would be for a few days at his father's house, and that she must not worry about his absence.

CHAPTER XVIII

———⇒➤●≪———

The Decision

A WEEK AFTER the duel, Paul Beaurepas sent each of his cousins, by old Terence, a written invitation to dine at the family mansion on Royal Street. The physical wounds were sufficiently healed to permit their attendance, though Raoul wore a scar on his cheek, Hector wore a bit of plaster on his ear, and Henri walked with a cane. Their spirits, however, were still sore, and had they dared, they would have declined the invitation. With the exception of Philippe, despite their outward mask of deference, not one of them but hated the interloper with a sullen fury, all the more venomous because futile. But the invitation had all the force of a command. Paul Beaurepas was their creditor. He had intimated in his letter that this interview would fix the relations which should exist in the future between him and his new found cousins, to whom it was of prime importance that these relations should be friendly.

The beautiful dining room, decorated in the style of

Louis Quinze, with mirrors between the tall windows, and figures around the ceiling, molded in stucco, lighted by a vast chandelier filled with wax candles, had been freshly renovated for the occasion. There were bunches of roses on the table, which was set with the family plate, in part inherited, and in part imported by old Pierre at the time of his marriage many years before. The menu exhausted the art of the Creole kitchen, which was famous for culinary excellence, and was served by old Terence, assisted by a deft-handed, light-footed mulatto boy.

There was at the beginning a certain air of constraint among the cousins, which Paul did his best to lighten. They had been surprised and humiliated by the result of the meeting at The Oaks, and were wondering whether their kinsman[1] might not have some further fantastic scheme of revenge to spring upon them. Since the meeting, they no longer had any doubts—if they had ever had any based on anything but self-interest—about the descent and racial purity of the *çi-devant* quadroon. He had proved his blood by his deeds—and they liked to think that any one of them could have done the same thing in his place. It was worthy of a Beaurepas.

But they were manifestly uneasy. Philippe was perhaps the least disturbed. His participation in the duel had been indeed a "mere formality," he having given his cousin no cause of offense; and in such of the family conferences as had taken place since then, he had played, so far as loyalty to his brother and his other cousins would permit, the part of peacemaker. They would gain nothing, he argued, by a bellicose attitude. They were absolutely at their cousin Paul's mercy. It would be impossible to break the will, and, if they spoke their new found kinsman fair, he might deal leniently, perhaps even generously, with them.

For, when all was said, he was a Beaurepas, and the pride of family which he had already displayed would no doubt stretch to include his cousins. He had been given the satisfaction of a gentleman for his fancied insults. He was the head of the family, and one cannot be a head without a following. In business, in public life, should he choose to enter it, and especially on the new social sea upon which he must now seek to float, the good will of his five cousins could not but be of value. It was true that he could crush them, but would it be wise or prudent to do so? Bankrupt, discredited, they would be worth nothing to him. But so long as they could hold up their heads, they were still in the forefront of Creole society. They could put him up at clubs and introduce him to the best people, and in politics their clan support would be an important asset.

As the meal progressed, however, and the wine went round, some of the constraint wore off. The guests told stories of social happenings, which they supposed might, from their novelty to him, be of interest to their host. They detailed the more or less scandalous gossip of the clubs and gaming houses, and the rumors of the cotton market and the stock exchange. They discussed the French company which was playing in repertory at the New Orleans Theater. The opera and the quadroon ball were not mentioned—it was an excellent policy to let sleeping dogs lie.

When the coffee had been served and Terence had decanted and set before them several bottles of the vintage Burgundy which old Pierre had imported twenty years before, Paul Marchand's face grew grave, he seemed preoccupied, and an air of anxious expectation settled upon the face of his guests. Finally the host rose and spoke.

"Gentlemen and cousins," he said, "in pursuance of the suggestion conveyed to you in my letter, I have summoned you here tonight with a twofold purpose—first, to return, as well as I may, your courtesy and hospitality so cordially tendered me upon my accession to my inheritance, and, secondly, to make a fitting response to your offer of friendship and fealty. The first you may consider done; I am proud to welcome you, as host, to a table where you were at home before I was, and I appreciate to the full what must seem to you the hard fate which gives to me what any one of you might well have anticipated as his own.

"I find myself in a unique and difficult position—one absolutely novel, so far as I can learn, in the history of Louisiana. Doubtless there have been unfortunate white children whose parents have abandoned them to nameless obscurity. But never before, I like to think, has the legitimate son of a good family been condemned by his parents to an inferior class solely to gratify a woman's selfish pride and a man's sentimental weakness—if not callous indifference—and then, after many years, been recalled to his own race and family.

"I need not dwell upon the moral and spiritual aspects of a quadroon's life. A little imagination, it seems to me, ought to make them vivid enough. They are too painful to dwell upon, but such as they are, I suffered them.

"While doing so, I condemned the laws and customs which degraded me, and would have changed them if I could. Nor have I altered my views. A man whose opinions upon a vital subject differ from those of the majority, and who would not play the part of a coward by denying or concealing or living counter to his convictions, could not live usefully or happily, if he could live at all, in Louisiana. Some day these laws will pass, these customs change—I hope the change will not come, as it did in France or in the island across the Gulf, in a deluge of blood, but come it will, if not in our time, then in that of our children. Could I by remaining here advance that day, I would do so gladly."

Does he mean, thought the cousins, to sell out and move away, taking with him our chief claim to financial credit and social distinction, the family fortune, and all for a mawkish negrophile sentiment? It would be a base, a dastardly thing to do!

"And I have still another embarrassment," Paul went on. "Under the former misconception as to my condition, I married a free woman of color. She brought me the larger freedom which wealth brings in some degree even to a quadroon. She has made me a faithful and devoted wife and has borne me two bright and beautiful children. What is her position under the laws of Louisiana? While I was supposedly a quadroon, she was an honored wife, they were legitimate children, if only those of a man of color; now she is nothing—a light woman, a *mulâtresse*,[2] and they are simply a gentleman's by-blows.

"I have spoken, as you have spoken, of the honor of the Beaurepas. Is it honor to forswear a solemn obligation, assumed with the sanction of God and man—for these our marriage had until a few weeks since? Is it honorable to abandon one's children to a nameless and hopeless future, as my parents so long abandoned me? Would it be honorable to keep them in any other relationship than that of honest and open family life? To me it would seem the depth of dishonor. I must confess, gentlemen, that my father's experiment has proved a failure.

"My cousin Henri once said, quite truthfully, in my hearing, though the remark was not addressed to me, that blood without breeding cannot make a gentleman. It may be said with equal truth that the race consciousness which is the strongest of the Creole characteristics, is not a matter of blood alone, but in large part the product of education and environment; it is social rather than personal. A man cannot, at my age, change easily his whole outlook upon life, nor can one trained as quadroon become overnight a—Beaurepas. In New Orleans, where a man must be of one caste or another, where there is no place for the individual as such, I, who have been all my life without father or mother, now find myself, in sympathy, without a race. In other words, gentlemen, Monsieur Pierre Beaurepas has bequeathed me a pair of seven league boots which do not fit, and which I cannot wear. It is the culminating tragedy of my life thus far that I can find no pleasure in the headship of this fine old family, with all its opportunities for development and usefulness, and I can feel no spark of filial love, or tenderness for a father whom I never knew, and a mother who repented of and dreaded my existence.

"What then, gentlemen? Fortunately there is a way out, which more than one white man of New Orleans has taken before, as well as some of our quadroon kinsmen. In a very short time I shall leave New Orleans and move with my family to France, where men are judged by their worth and not by their color, where in all honor my wife can be my wife and my children, my children, and I need not be ashamed of them nor they afraid of me."

His voice had been affected by emotion, and while he lifted his glass to moisten his lips, the cousins regarded one another dolefully. Their worst fears were realized. Gone would soon be the wealth and prestige of the family, and they would be left mere ordinary Creoles, of mediocre parts and financially on the rocks! But their cousin had not finished.

"Certain notes were given by you gentlemen to your late uncle," he went on, "for money loaned, and have come to me as part of the inheritance. They have, I think, served their purpose. They were intended, I believe, to deceive, and had that effect—they were given as suggested advancements, and received in that light. They were meant to place you in my power and have done so; but as I am in no danger from you, and have no designs against you, and only wish you well, I take pleasure in returning them to you."

"That is generous of you, cousin," said Henri.

"Yes," added Raoul, "we thank you very much."

"The slaves belonging to the estate I shall manumit— that much of my prerogative as heir I shall exercise. I wish I could wipe out the system as easily—I consider it the sum of all villainies. The remainder of the property, in its entirety, I shall relinquish. I cannot hold it upon the conditions, expressed or implied, which Monsieur Pierre Beaurepas has made, nor could I in honor keep it otherwise."

The faces of the cousins reflected the joy to which this statement gave quick rise. If their cousin should renounce the inheritance, it would come to them by law, as their uncle's next of kin, in equal shares. One fifth of the estate would be a fortune for each. But this spark of hope was rudely extinguished, for all but one of them, by the speaker's next words.

"I shall transfer it, by proper legal conveyance," he continued, "to Monsieur Philippe Beaurepas, whom I have chosen as my successor, with the confident hope that he will use it for the honor and glory of a family which means so much to him and to you all and to Louisiana, but which, I say it sadly, can mean nothing to me. The honor that I fought you for the other day, was not the honor of the family; it was my own starved, my own maimed self-respect which clamored for satisfaction. I shall not even assume the family name—I would not bear the name of a man who would treat his son as Monsieur Pierre Beaurepas has treated me."

It was apparent that the iron had entered Paul Beaurepas's soul very deeply. The cousins recalled, later on, when they were talking over this meeting—as Don José Morales had observed upon a previous occasion—that rarely had Paul referred to their uncle as his father. Before anyone could speak Paul Beaurepas resumed: "And now, gentlemen, I give you the health of Monsieur Philippe Beaurepas, your cousin, *our* cousin, the heir of the estate and the head of the family."

They were so dazed by their host's announcement that they drank the toast in silence. Presently Philippe, having recovered somewhat from his amazement, rose to his feet.

"Cousin," he said, his voice faltering with emotion, "you have taken us all by surprise—me most of all. You have been shabbily treated, and you have taken generous revenge. Despite your disclaimer, you have maintained the honor of the family upon the loftiest plane. I know no other man who would be capable of what you are about to do—I know that I should not. Words are inadequate, even could I command them, to express my gratitude. I can only say that I shall try to wear my honors worthily, and shall regard the property as a trust to be administered in a manner that will conform to my uncle's wishes and meet with your approval and be a credit to the family and to humanity. And I shall, as no doubt you would wish, extend to my brother and my other cousins all proper kinsmansly devotion. You have opened to me, cousin, by your munificence, a future which is all bright. And I wish you and yours, in your distant home, all the happiness which you have placed it in my power to achieve for myself and another who is dear to me."

"Among the assets I shall turn over to you, dear cousin," resumed Paul, with a tender smile—was it tinged with regret?—"is the mortgage on Trois Pigeons on condition that you settle it in the manner your uncle intended."

"It is the greatest gift of all," returned Philippe, gratefully. "I think my uncle meant her for a better man, but I will take her and be thankful. I have loved her all her life."

Paul had meant to terminate the interview at this point. He had made his great renunciation and touched the dramatic climax of the play. He had dealt, he thought, generously with his kinsmen. Philippe had spoken from the heart. The others had thanked him with their lips, but he could read from their faces that, freed from the menace of their outstanding debts and with nothing further to hope for, they frankly hated him for his preference of Philippe, and Philippe because he had been preferred. So he hardened his heart and shot his last bolt—it would strike Philippe as well, but he must take the bitter with the sweet—the others must not escape.

"I have one thing more to say," said Paul. "It concerns a matter involving, radically, the standing of the family. I have hesitated to speak of it, but I think, as representatives of a proud house and a proud race, you ought to know it. In looking through the late Monsieur Pierre Beaurepas's papers, I discovered incontestable proof that one of the five children who were brought to New Orleans from San Domingo, one, though also a cousin, was of quadroon birth. The five children who came from San Domingo grew up into you five gentlemen. The corollary is obvious.

"I thought it no more than your right to know this. And whether you shall learn any more I leave to you. It had occurred to me that you might desire, for the sake of racial purity and the family honor, to expel this cuckoo from the nest, this intruder from your midst; that you might not wish longer to meet on terms of kinship and equality this baseborn interloper, who— through no fault of his own, it is true, and in all ignorance, but nonetheless unlawfully—is exercising the rights and privileges of a wellborn white man. Since I am going away and have no longer any direct personal interest, I feel no responsibility in the matter. Gentlemen, I leave it to you whether I shall name the man. Shall I or shall I not?"

The cousins were dazed, if possible, more completely than before. They had supposed their capacity for astonishment exhausted, but this announcement had sounded new depths. They looked at one another furtively, and studied their own reflections in the mirrors which lined the walls of the dining room. One perceived in another a certain breadth of the nostril, but in himself a certain fullness of lip—in one a certain thickness of eyelid, in himself a certain wave of the hair. They examined their fingernails furtively for the telltale black streak. For a moment no one spoke.

"Which shall it be, gentlemen?" asked Paul softly. "Yes or no?"

The answer came as one voice.

"No!"

"I think you have chosen wisely," said Paul, suavely, "and I assure you that the secret shall remain locked in my own bosom."

There was a happy woman in the house on Bourbon Street a little later in the evening. Julie's fears were dissipated, an honorable future for herself and her children assured.

In another land, where kindlier customs prevailed, Paul Marchand prospered in business, and reared a family of sons and daughters, some of whom distinguished themselves in various walks of life. A son, a lieutenant in the French Navy, came to the United States in 1863. He was attached as an observation officer, to Admiral Farragut's staff, and was present at the taking of the city of New Orleans. Philippe Beaurepas, then past middle life, and later one of the first reconstructed rebels, entertained him at dinner in the old house on Royal Street, where he still lived, though in diminished state, for while the honor of the family proved safe in Philippe's hands, he was not a good business man and the family fortune had sadly dwindled. He had married Josephine Morales, and their union had proved a happy one. They lived in the family mansion and kept Trois Pigeons as a country place. They named their first son Paul.

It might be supposed that the fact disclosed to Paul's cousins at the second dinner, as to the origin of some one of them, would have made them more tolerant of those of darker blood. But, with the exception of Philippe, it had the contrary effect. Henri was killed in a duel, Adolphe died of yellow fever, but the survivors and descendants, some of whom achieved prominence in public life, were ever in the forefront of any agitation to limit the rights or restrict the privileges of their darker fellow citizens. They helped procure the passage of a law forbidding the manumission of slaves and lead an abortive movement to expel all free colored people from Louisiana. They fought gallantly for slavery in the Civil

War, were leaders and advisers of the Ku Klux Klan, and prominent in the "redemption" of Louisiana and the nullification of the Fifteenth Amendment. A grandson of Henri Beaurepas not long since introduced into the Louisiana legislature an amendment to the criminal code, making marriage a felony between a white person and person of colored blood to the thirty-second degree inclusive. One wonders if he had ever learned of the ancestral possibility.

NOTES TO
PAUL MARCHAND, F.M.C.

A GENERAL NOTE ON EDITING
FOR CONSISTENCY

CHESNUTT was inconsistent in handling certain details of punctuation and spelling. Sometimes he conforms to the practices of an earlier era, and sometimes in the same text he follows modern practice. To give two examples: Chesnutt frequently separates contracted words—"does n't," "would n't"—and he sometimes follows a dash with other punctuation; however, he follows neither of these practices in all cases. In the interest of consistency, I have chosen, in these instances, to follow contemporary practice; thus contracted words are not separated, and there is no punctuation after dashes in the manuscript I have prepared.

Chesnutt is also inconsistent in handling the title "Monsieur" when it is used with a given name or a family name. Sometimes he spells the title in full, and sometimes he uses the abbreviation "M." Although modern editorial practice encourages the abbreviated form, I feel that "M." with a name in an English text risks being misread as an initial. Moreover, names and titles are particularly important in this novel of status and identity; thus I have chosen to spell out in all instances "Monsieur," "Madame," and "Mademoiselle."

FOREWORD

1. George Washington Cable (1844–1925) was the most successful author of Louisiana local-color fiction. His portraits of pre–Civil War New Orleans gained a wide national audience, but his critical attitude toward certain aspects of the South, especially the condition of the Negro, forced him to settle in the North, where he became a leader among whites sympathetic to the Negro cause. In 1899 Cable offered Chesnutt a post as his personal secretary. Chesnutt declined, but the men remained friends and allies. For the Chesnutt-Cable correspondence, see *"To Be an Author,"* 29–72. Cable's closest rival as a Louisiana local colorist was Grace L. King (1851–1932). King was also Cable's ideological opponent. A descendant of the pre–Civil War Louisiana aristocracy, she claimed she began writing to defend the old order against Cable's criticisms.

CHAPTER I

1. Grace King describes Zabet Philosophe, a well-known figure in early-nineteenth-century New Orleans. This freed slave "took to selling pralines on the steps of the cathedral, or under the porch of the Cabildo, where she could see her friends, the judges and lawyers, as they passed on their way to court; and they seldom failed to loiter around her tray to provoke from her the shrewd comments, piquante stories and picturesque tales which won her the surname of Philosophe" (339).

CHAPTER II

1. The manuscript has "Hector," but it was Raoul Beaurepas who insulted Paul Marchand in front of the cathedral.

2. I have edited and punctuated this passage for clarity. Here is the original: For how could any man, unless he were a hero, or a martyr to a cause—and Marchand was neither,—how could any one move with dignity among those in whose presence one had just been called a pig and had another threaten to slit his ears, nay, even announce that his touch would be a pollution, if but for the purpose of performing upon him a surgical operation which even a gentleman might presumably perform upon a pig, without defilement!—when the conditions were such that he might not resent the insult?

CHAPTER IV

1. The song "Delaide, mo la reine" was transcribed and published by William Head Coleman (153–60).

CHAPTER V

1. The Duc de Nemours (1814–96) was the second son of Louis-Philippe I, who reigned as King of France from 1830 to 1848. I have found no record of the Duc de Nemours ever visiting New Orleans. He would, moreover, have been a child in 1821 when the novel is set. His father, then the Duc d'Orleans, did visit the city while in North American exile during the French revolutionary period. The most likely historical analogue to the novel's duke, however, was the Duke of Saxe-Weimar, who visited the city in 1825 and who recorded his impressions of the Quadroon Balls in his journal. Grace King describes his visit to New Orleans and the Quadroon Ball (343).

2. Louis Moreau Gottschalk was born in 1829 and died in 1869; thus his composition could not have been performed in 1821.

Chapter VI

1. The manuscript has "señora," but Josephine is not married.

Chapter VIII

1. The manuscript has "kinsmen."

Chapter X

1. The manuscript has "vicegerency."

Chapter XI

1. The manuscript has "latter."

Chapter XIV

1. Grace King describes The Oaks and the Creole cult of dueling (290–97).

Chapter XVIII

1. The manuscript has "kinsmen," but the reference is to Paul Beaurepas.

2. The manuscript has "*milatresse*." *Mulâtresse*, in standard French and in the Louisiana French dialect, means a woman of mixed European and African ancestry.

WORKS CITED

Andrews, William L. *The Literary Career of Charles W. Chesnutt*. Baton Rouge: Louisiana State University Press, 1980.

Baker, Houston A., Jr. *Modernism and the Harlem Renaissance*. Chicago: University of Chicago Press, 1987.

Chesnutt, Charles W. *The Colonel's Dream*. Upper Saddle River, NJ: Gregg Press, 1968.

——. *The Conjure Woman*. Ann Arbor: University of Michigan Press, 1969.

——. "Hand of God." Unpublished story. Chesnutt Collection. Western Historical Society Library. Cleveland, Ohio.

——. *The House Behind the Cedars*. New York: Penguin, 1993.

——. *The Journals of Charles W. Chesnutt*. Ed. Richard Brodhead. Durham, NC: Duke University Press, 1993.

——. Letter to Alfred A. Knopf, Esq. 20 December 1921. Chesnutt Collection. Fisk University Library.

——. Letter to Houghton Mifflin Company, 8 October 1921. Chesnutt Collection. Fisk University Library.

——. Letter to Harcourt Brace and Company. 12 November 1921. Chesnutt Collection. Fisk University Library.

——. *Mandy Oxendine*. Ed. Charles Hackenberry. Urbana: University of Illinois Press, 1997.

——. *The Marrow of Tradition*. New York: Penguin, 1993.

——. *The Short Fiction of Charles W. Chesnutt*. Ed. Sylvia

Lyons Render. Washington, DC: Howard University Press, 1981.

———. *The Wife of His Youth and Other Stories*. Ann Arbor: University of Michigan Press, 1968.

———. *"To Be an Author": Letters of Charles W. Chesnutt*. Ed. Joseph R. McElrath, Jr., and Robert C. Leitz, III. Princeton: Princeton University Press, 1997.

Chesnutt, Helen. *Charles Waddell Chesnutt: Pioneer of the Color Line*. Chapel Hill: University of North Carolina Press, 1952.

Coleman, William Head. *Historical Sketch Book and Guide to New Orleans*. New York: W. H. Coleman, 1885.

Dominguez, Virginia R. *White by Definition: Social Classification in Creole Louisiana*. New Brunswick, NJ: Rutgers University Press, 1986.

Gates, Henry Louis, Jr. *The Signifying Monkey: A Theory of African American Literary Criticism*. Oxford: Oxford University Press, 1988.

———, and Nellie Y. McKay, eds. *The Norton Anthology of African American Literature*. New York: Norton, 1997.

King, Grace. *New Orleans: The Place and the People*. New York: Macmillan, 1896.

Kunkle, Paul A. "Modifications in Louisiana Negro Legal Status, 1812–1957." *Journal of Negro History* 44 (1959): 1–25.

Lewis, David Levering. *When Harlem Was in Vogue*. New York: Oxford University Press, 1989.